PRAISE FOR KENNETH JOHNSON

"A haunting and unforgettable sojourn into uncertainty, and fear, with thrills along the way. A must read on your 2025 bookshelf or nightstand. Kept me rivetted for hours."

— *STRAND MAGAZINE*

"Kenneth Johnson sets the hook and reels us in while the characters struggle to navigate this utterly unique premise! Outstanding!"

— JONAS SAUL, BESTSELLING AUTHOR OF THE *SARAH ROBERTS SERIES*

"Kenneth Johnson's *The Face in the Mirror* ratchets up the tension from the first moment. A skillfully executed dark thriller that works its way into your psyche...in concert with the best works from Robert Bloch and William Peter Batty."

— JOHN PALISANO, BRAM STOKER AWARD-WINNING AUTHOR OF *REQUIEM* AND *GHOST HEART*

"Without question Kenneth Johnson is the closest our generation will come to the great Rod Serling. His understanding of the human mind has created some of the most developed and understood characters ever. When Kenneth Johnson puts something out, it is always quality."

— *SCAREDSTIFFREVIEWS.COM*

"Kenneth Johnson . . . knows how to make magic."

— *THE PHILADELPHIA INQUIRER*

"Kenneth Johnson is nothing less than phenomenal."

— *NIGHT OWL REVIEWS*

"Johnson channels Stephen King with this thriller... a nerve-wracking race to an unexpected conclusion."

— *BOOKLIST, ON DARWIN VARIANT*

"Johnson has written another engaging novel."

— *ASSOCIATED PRESS, ON DARWIN VARIANT*

"*V*—Victorious as sci-fi miniseries... Dazzling... An intelligent, imaginative, engrossing four-hour drama. *V* is a thought-provoking, sometimes shocking drama that keeps the viewer engaged."

— *NEW YORK DAILY NEWS, ON V*

"Right at the top we know that *V* isn't just another fling at science fiction—it is nothing less than a retelling of history —the rise of the Nazis done as a cautionary science fiction fable. For television this is probably a first."

— *THE NEW YORK TIMES, ON V*

" Kenneth Johnson... creates a rich and fully invented world, and makes it pay off with well-developed characters and an interesting perspective on our own culture... It's innovative."

— *THE WALL STREET JOURNAL, ON ALIEN NATION*

"First-rate entertainment . . . Much of the success probably has to do with the fact it was written, produced and directed by Kenneth Johnson."

— *THE SEATTLE TIMES, ON ALIEN NATION*

The Face in the Mirror

The Face in the Mirror

Kenneth Johnson

Cemetery Dance Publications
Baltimore
❧ 2025 ❧

For Herbert George Wells

*An enduring inspiration since
my childhood encounter
with his novels...*

*The Time Machine
and
The War of the Worlds*

Chapter 1

There was a frightening screech as automatic brakes slammed on, and the late-model Tesla skidded to a stop half an inch before hitting Matthew Shaw.

Matt was bent forward over the hood, hands atop the gunmetal-gray surface, heart pounding. He saw his own twenty-four-year-old face reflected in the windshield—wide-eyed and white with shock. The furious driver was shaking a fist and shouting Farsi epithets at the idiot pedestrian. Matt held up his hands, sincerely embarrassed. "Sorry, s-sorry!" he sputtered, his breath puffing in the chill November morning air.

Matt had trailed his gangly pal Dev Bhandari, dodging through New York's Lower Fifth Avenue traffic. Dev grabbed Matt's windbreaker sleeve and pulled him on toward the curb while calling out in his Gujarati dialect to the driver, "Pardon us, uncle!" Dev's other hand waved a small cooler labeled HUMAN ORGANS. "Medical emergency!"

The driver saw Dev's pile of black hair brushed straight up like a tall crown and took him to be equally idiotic. He snarled in Farsi—which likely translated as *I'll give you a goddamn medical emergency*—and swerved the weighty car right at them.

"Whoa!" Dev yelped as they leapt up onto the sidewalk, barely avoiding contact when the beefy front tire banged the curb and ricocheted off. The furious driver stabbed his middle finger at them and sped south toward Washington Square.

Matt's heart was fluttering from both near misses. "I *told* you, man!" he said with a mad-clown grin at his classmate. "We should've g-gone down to the light."

"You are right, as usual," Dev acknowledged, as they hurriedly navigated through the United Nations of people on the busy sidewalk, their pace as brisk as the kinetic energy of lower Manhattan life bustling around them. "But jaywalking offers unexpected excitement!"

"Excitement's okay. Survival's more important."

"Oh Mattsy, I am just trying to pump up your spirit of adventure." Dev spotted something ahead. "And look! There's your chance for some *safe* adventures!" He pointed enthusiastically toward a line of identical posters plastered on a plywood wall. They heralded a current event at Town Hall: BEYOND PARANORMAL WITH DR. THELMA GREER. The sixtyish face of Dr. Greer stared out piercingly through her slightly tinted glasses with a shrewdly raised eyebrow.

"Just look at her expression!" Dev gazed with starstruck eyes as they passed. "You can absolutely tell she really knows stuff. That she has seen some weird shit." Dev had the bubbling cheeriness of a true believer. "It's going to be so cool to see her live and—"

"Forget it, Bhandari," Matt interrupted, chuckling. "I didn't get into med school to study alien autopsies."

"We will *perform* one someday, mark my words."

"*You* probably will," Matt said wryly, "Right after you get abducted and probed."

Dev ignored him. "It's going to be a great convention. Lots of *Stranger Things* stuff! Plus, the new *Doctor Who*," he tapped one of Greer's poster faces, "and she's doing different panels about her years running UCLA's Parapsych Unit, all her great poltergeist hunting and—"

"Dev!" Matt jerked his friend to a momentary stop in front of the last poster with imposing Dr. Greer staring right at them. "Try to focus." Other grumbling pedestrians dodged around them as Matt used both hands for emphasis. "We are at NYU. Not Roswell U."

"Matt!" Dev deftly imitated his friend's emphasis, standing his ground. "*You* have got to open your mind, expand your thinking. '*There are more things in Heaven and Earth, Horatio*—'"

"Than in my bank account," Matt countered, then shivered from the cold as they walked on. "Buying food is higher on my list than seeing fuzzy photos of UFOs."

"Okay, okay." Dev kept pace, shouting to be heard as an FDNY paramedic van sped past with emergency horn blaring, "But you really need to spend a couple bucks on a Thermoball, Mattsy." He was referencing his own bright yellow North Face jacket which was much more protective than Matt's frail windbreaker. "And listen, if food is the issue, I have got you covered." He opened the HUMAN ORGANS cooler while they hurried along and pulled out a clear Ziploc bag containing a chunk of human liver.

Matt spoke deadpan—as if he took it seriously. "I've told you, Dev: no red meat."

"Just as well," Dev said as he put it away. "The pathology team wouldn't want it if you'd taken a bite. But how about—?" He pulled a banana from the cooler and wiggled it at Matt.

Matt shook his head, laughing. "How about you get your ass in gear so we're not late?"

Across the avenue from them, nestled among pedestrians who were headed in the same direction as Matt and Dev, a man was slightly ahead of them, but keeping pace.

Anyone glancing at him would not have looked twice. He was in his fifties, from central European stock. The well-worn baseball cap over his salt-and-pepper buzz cut had no team logo. His green, vintage US Marine's peacoat looked exactly like millions of others.

He was nondescript. That was his preferred appearance when working.

He was looking straight ahead as he walked, however, he repeatedly glanced down at the small video screen on the device in his hand. It had been specifically designed to resemble a satellite phone, including the heavy-duty cylindrical antenna, an inch in diameter and six inches long, common to sat phones. But it was not an antenna. It was a highly directional microphone with sensitivity and technology far beyond anything available to anyone without a security clearance.

His handheld device was a sophisticated digital camera designed for clandestine surveillance. He had its disguised, ultra-compact lens pointed across the avenue. Displayed on its screen was a head-to-toe image of Dev and Matt. A blinking red dot indicated that it was recording. The observer holding it continued tracking them as they walked.

Two blocks above Washington Square, the two collegians turned east onto East Ninth Street, then skittered across to the south sidewalk. The observer paused his recorder, moved across Fifth Avenue. Adroitly skirting a two-deck sightseeing bus, he kept the two students in view. Following them discreetly from the north sidewalk of Ninth, he steered smoothly between slower pedestrians to get slightly ahead of his targets. He then restarted his recording as they approached a repurposed 1950s office building just before University Place. It featured a modern sign with a black glass background and stainless-steel lettering, identifying it as MED-X LABORATORIES. Several employees were in a short line at the security entrance. Dev fell in behind them, but Matt was looking around for someone.

The observer also slowed to a stop slightly past them on his opposite side of the street and leaned casually against a lamp post. He never glanced in their direction but kept watching their images on his video screen. He saw Matt continue to scan around and for a moment Matt looked directly into his camera. The observer didn't budge but watched his screen as he pretended to be tapping it in his hand. He was certain Matt would assume he was deeply engaged in something on his sat phone. He was correct. Matt's gaze passed right on as he stepped off the curb to peer further down the street. Then he called back to Dev, loudly enough for the observer to hear.

"Hey Dev, do you see her back toward Fifth? She said she really wanted to—"

"Matty! Hey!" a female voice shouted. Matt turned around to look towards University Place.

The observer's handheld camera followed Matt's turn, panning to find and focus on a striking, sunny-faced young woman who'd appeared from around the corner on the observer's side. He recognized her immediately from his team's earlier surveillances and research.

He knew Molly Perez was twenty-five. Her rich auburn hair and hazel eyes indicated that her mother from Ireland's County Cork had possessed the strongest gene pool. Her father's Argentine heritage contributed the warming color to her smooth skin. She was bundled against the cold in a white, puffy down coat over a purple NYU sweatshirt. She jaywalked quickly across Ninth, gracefully dodging a fast-moving e-scooter messenger and a Subaru Uber to reach Matt.

The HD videocam zoomed in closer as Molly gave Matt a quick kiss and fist-bumped Dev. The observer was confident they were unaware of his surveillance. Since Ninth Street was much narrower than Fifth Avenue, he was able to fine-tune his directional mike, filtering out much of the ambient city noise, distant sirens and such. He knew an occasional passing vehicle would momentarily interrupt the signal to his earbuds, but he'd be able to get the gist of their conversation. He settled in to observe and heard Molly eagerly asking Matt, "Did you have time to read it?"

The observer's seasoned eyes noticed a very subtle—but to him telltale—shift in Matt's expression. He saw that Dev, standing in line behind them, also sensed Matt's trepidation.

After the briefest pause Matt said, "Yeah." He sounded generally positive as he pulled a few wrinkled pages from within his worn, thin jacket. "Yeah, Moll. It's good. I liked it."

"You did!" She bounced slightly, relieved. "I'm so glad!"

She hugged him, crushing the papers between them while enthusiastically talking a mile a minute. "I dug really deep into interviews with people who were *on* Pettus Bridge that Bloody Sunday. People on John Lewis's side, but also sheriff's deputies who attacked. I found firsthand details I'd never heard! It was so terrifying and brave and historic all at once!" She looked keenly into Matt's blue eyes, seeking affirmation. "And you liked how I blended it all?"

"Yes. It's a good essay." His smile was genuine, but also—the observer felt—it was a bit wan. Molly also sensed Matt's subtle hesitancy as he went on, "It's r-really well-written, but…"

Molly's shoulders sagged. Matt's stutter apparently betrayed his uneasiness, confirming her suspicions. Her eyebrows went up. She stuck the word right back at him, "*But…?*"

"Well," Dev intervened loudly, eager to avoid the line of fire, "My *personal butt* is freezing off. And—" he lifted the Human Organs container "—I've got to get this into the path team. Catch you later, Molly." He escaped into the lab building as Matt felt the pressure of Molly's stare.

"Didn't you say your assignment was to be 'c-completely objective'?"

Molly frowned, annoyed. "It *is* objective! I patterned it after Hemingway's early dispatches from the Spanish Civil War. I was really careful to stay unemotional, not editorialize and—" She cut herself off with a huff, looked away from his steady gaze. Stewing about his implied criticism.

Matt averted his own eyes, giving her room to go through her irritation. Then Matt said softly, "Here's what I honestly think, Moll: It really is some of your f-finest writing. You drew me inside those horrible moments and—"

"Oh pu-*leeze*," she waved a hand dismissively, "don't try to backpedal and—"

"Just listen a sec, huh?"

She planted her weight on one foot with a huff of irritation and stood hipshot. Without looking at him she popped her head archly, indicating for him to continue. If he must.

The observer allowed a slight smile to curl one corner of his lips. Despite his professional detachment and inbred cynicism, he was intrigued by this young couple's interaction.

Matt spoke quietly. "The way you assembled all the pieces is powerful, Moll. There were a couple places, though, wh-where I found myself remembering what you told me this *same* professor had said—"

"About what?" she snapped.

"About reading between the lines to learn whose side the writer is on." Matt saw her eyes flick slightly, her mind opening a crack. "By examining which *adjectives* a writer chooses." He pointed at a sentence. "Like here, where you wrote, 'When the coldhearted attack began, John Lewis and his marchers heroically stood their ground—'"

Molly's taut face slackened suddenly. "Oh, shit." The observer saw she was busted, and she knew it. She tried to fight down a smile, wanted to hold onto her anger, but couldn't. A laugh percolated out as she repeated, with mortified enlightenment, "Shit." She nodded.

The observer had also understood and nodded as Molly articulated, "Writing 'coldhearted' and 'heroically' tips off my own subjective feelings."

"Which most people agree are exactly the *right* feelings," Matt encouraged.

"But the specific assignment was for me *not* to express any opinion. Only unbiased reportage." She chuckled, finally looked into his eyes, embarrassed by her annoyance. She took her papers from his hand. "I'll weed back through it, make sure there's not too much of me in it."

"Could never be too much for me, Moll."

She touched the lock of chestnut hair on his forehead. "You are sooo—I'm searching for the perfect, highly-biased adjective—*sweet!*"

She gave him a very real kiss. The observer noticed a fifty-something woman of Middle Eastern descent passing by them who saw their kiss and smiled as she continued inside. Then Molly snuggled Matt but grew concerned. "Oh Matty, you're cold. We've got to get you a warmer coat."

He shrugged it off. "I'll survive till my next paycheck. See you tonight?"

"Yeah. And thanks for being honest." He was happy to have helped. She leaned closer again, with a bedroom smile. "And tonight… Definitely."

After a quick parting kiss, she headed off happily. Matt gazed fondly after her before entering the lab.

The observer clicked off his surveillance camera. He stood contemplatively for a moment as the traffic on Ninth Street continued passing and New York pedestrians of varying shapes, sizes, and ethnicities hurried by in both directions. He was weighing the professional need to remain unbiased himself.

Finally, the observer inhaled a resolute breath. He walked back toward Fifth Avenue, blending in among the populace and feeling that at least the time of information gathering was ended. The harvest had been plentiful.

In less than a day, he could proceed to the final stage of his mission.

~~~~

MATT WAS PLEASED TO HAVE GOTTEN HIS JOB AT MED-X ten months earlier. It was not only his prime source of income, but a prestigious credit to have on his CV because Med-X was the prime biochemical facility affiliated with NYU hospitals and health centers. Matt went through the small public lobby, then used his ID card to enter the cloak room for storing outdoor garments. Still chilled from being outside, he left his windbreaker on and put a fresh white lab coat over it. He paused before opening the security door into the ground floor laboratory. He took a deep preparatory breath. That had become a ritual for him: readying himself for what lay ahead.

Matt's ID opened the door, and it hit him full in the face, just as it always did.

The Whiteness.

After working in the lab ten months—even ten *years*, some longtime employees had told him—the white-out effect was still phenomenal. Everything in the room was white: the walls, floor and ceiling with its abundant built-in LED illumination.

About three-fourths the size of an all-white basketball court, the laboratory's whiteness was overwhelming. The first time Matt walked into the lab he'd thought even the air seemed white. And smelled white.

Long, clean, white countertops at desk height lined the walls. Below them were multi-sized white drawers containing supplies. Every four feet there were leg spaces for workers seated on white chairs or stools.

Above the countertops were easily reachable white shelves containing white electronic instruments as well as racks of glass test tubes, bottles, vials, volumetric flasks in all imaginable sizes and often quirky shapes. Matt thought several were amusing, looking like nonsensical props from 1931's *Frankenstein*.

The fifty or so people working in the lab had faces of different colors, which leant a warm, humanizing aspect that Matt was grateful for, even though they were all clothed in white lab coats, some in matching white scrub pants. Many had white hair covers.

Staffers worked along the countertops operating many examples of sophisticated state-of-the-art, mostly white equipment. They were varying instruments for the analysis of blood components, enzymology, toxicology, endocrinology, DNA, and such. Everything Matt and others needed to study, document, and report lab tests from pathological research projects and health care patients.

Once acclimated to the initial blizzard of arctic whiteness, Matt also appreciated the grace notes of color sprinkled across the lab, such as the colorful LED touchscreens mounted over the eyepieces of the two dozen Koehler 40X-1000X Trinocular microscopes being used by skilled scientists. Plus, there were computer monitors of differing sizes displaying texts, graphs, oscillating 3D wireframe images of DNA and a few screensavers of landscapes, personal photos or, of course, cats.

The staff ranged in age from seniors down to college grads and med students like him and Dev.

Down the center of the room were two islands of white-topped lab tables with attending stools. Matt saw that Dr. Pauline Diamond, who had passed him and Molly outside, was settling in at her supervisory station. Pauline was a substantial, confident woman whom he knew was of Israeli heritage via Brooklyn. Early on, she'd treated him to a slice of cheesecake from Junior's on Flatbush Avenue. She extracted an iPad from her weathered carpet bag as Matt sat nearby to boot up a computer saying, "Good morning, Dr. D."

She smiled, glancing sideways at him as she started her iPad. "Looked like you were having a good morning outside."

Matt felt his cheeks redden as he smiled shyly, but proud. "… Yeah."

"A significant other perhaps?"

"I'm a lucky guy."

"I'd say she's pretty lucky, too. She at Tisch? Studying acting?"

Matt laughed lightly. "Double major in History-Journalism. But she gets asked that a lot."

"Understandable, with those looks." Pauline noticed he was fishing out his package of Tums. "Hey, you've been hitting those quite a bit. Feeling okay?"

"Physiology midterm next week." He drew a breath, looking away, thoughtful.

He knew she was watching him, likely sensing he was screwing up his courage about something as the lab around them continued buzzing with activity, analysis equipment bleeping, colleagues conversing. Finally, Matt said softly, "Also, Dr. D, I r-really hate to ask, but could I pick up a couple more hours here?"

She blinked. "With *your* load of classes? And also—"

"I'm doing okay academically," he jumped in, eager to quell her concern. "I really think I could handle it."

"But Jesus, Matt, between processing lab reports and doing IT for us, you're almost full time now. When will you sleep?"

He shrugged. "I figure maybe when I'm thirty-two."

Pauline leaned closer, her warm brown eyes peering over her hornrims. She spoke confidentially. "Is money that tight, kiddo?" He offered a pallid smile. She sighed. "I'll see what I can do with HR."

"That'd be great, I really appreciate—"

"Hey, Cyberman!" Dev called out.

They looked two tables away and saw that Dev had pulled a

white hair cover over his tall pile of black hair. It resembled a white top hat.

"Oh my God." Pauline chuckled. "*The Cat in the Hat* lives." Matt grinned as she asked, "Why *does* he brush his hair up like that?"

"He likes having a 'signature look.'" Matt grinned. "So why not? He's very proud of it—and it's sort of like having a pet."

Dev was pointing at his computer with serious concern. "Is the lymphatic cell analyzer program really supposed to look like *Mortal Kombat?*"

Pauline exhaled a frustrated puff. "Shit. Another goddamn virus?"

Matt was already on the move, waving back at her. "That one's easy-peasy. I'll inoculate it."

"You are the man, Matt!" Dev said much too loudly, for the doctor's benefit. "I will bet they pay you lots extra for all these viruses you save them from, huh Matt?"

Pauline smirked back, "Now there's an idea!" She gave Matt a wink and made a note on her iPad.

Matt poked his pal's shoulder. "Jeez, couldn't you say it a little louder?"

"Just trying to help, man. 'The squeaky wheel gets the oil.'"

"An old Indian saying?"

"Actually, it's a Bhandari original." He stood and Matt took the stool, eyeing the misbehaving computer screen as Dev shook his head. "I can't get back in."

"I thought guys from Mumbai were born knowing this stuff."

"My DNA was glitchy."

Matt's fingers were trying different combinations of multiple keys, but the animated images onscreen persisted. Matt muttered, "Actually this one looks more like *God of War.*" He tried two more combinations then suddenly the white-on-black DOS Command Prompt screen appeared.

"Ha!" Dev laughed. "You are a cybernetic sorcerer! The Fauci of IT." Then Dev spoke louder in Dr. Diamond's direction. "Wow, great save, Matt! You fixed another one!"

Matt was amused, but hissed at his pal, "Will you shut up?"

"Hey, when you've got it, flaunt it. But just remember when they pay you more—I get some vig."

Matt let Dev resume the stool and nodded. "Ten percent. Most def."

~~~~

THE OBSERVER WAS IN HIS MIDDLE-CLASS OFFICE ON THE lower West Side. Typical desktop items included a small container for business cards with his name, CHARLES REINHARDT, and his area of expertise, INVESTIGATIONS.

Reinhardt also wanted visitors to see authentication of his background experience, so his walls included mementos from years in military and FBI intelligence, then later educating recruits at Quantico before he'd taken early retirement and gone private.

Also in evidence were four new file folders. Clipped to the corner of each was a small photo of a different graduate student. The first, labeled Z-1, was a black male with neat dreads pulled tight in back, creating a ponytail. Z-2 was a male with red hair and freckles. Z-3 was a serious-looking female of perhaps Arabic heritage. Z-4 was Matthew Shaw.

Reinhardt was making a final editorial pass on the surveillance videos of Matt that he and his staff had recorded.

A twenty-four-inch monitor displayed the image of a burger joint called Cozy's. It was appropriately named, being a tiny, thirty-foot-wide mom-and-pop eatery nestled in the shadow of a looming, thirty-five-story apartment building at Broadway and Astor Place.

The video zoomed in through the window to frame on Matt and Dev sitting at the counter as a black waitress with purple hair joked with her old friends. She served Matt a bowl of Cozy's legendary pea soup and Dev a burger the size of Cleveland. Matt took a Tums then enjoyed the soup. The image froze.

Reinhardt dropped that shot into the montage timeline then continued playing the sequence of surveillance shots he had strung together. All were scenes of Matt living his everyday life. One showed Matt sitting with Dev and two female classmates on the concrete benches in front of Washington Square's classic Roman arch. Dev and the women were arguing over a complex passage in a medical textbook. Their words were audible but incomprehensible to anyone not steeped in medical terminology, including Reinhardt. One female pounded the page with her forefinger, heatedly expressed her interpretation and Dev stood up shouting, "What, are you *crazy*? How can how can you possibly *believe* that?" The offended woman jumped to her feet angrily, gathered her books and purse, preparing to storm off in a huff—when Matt muttered something unintelligible, but apparently so startling that the others stopped dead to stare at him.

Then they all cracked up, laughing heartily together at his comment. The tension evaporated. The female who'd been angry plopped back down, still laughing. The other young woman patted Matt's shoulder, appreciating his clever, understated ability to smooth the moment and right their ship with a single quip.

Reinhardt was impressed when he'd first seen that moment and he still was.

The next video was in Battery Park. Captured through a telephoto lens, with children crisscrossing the foreground, Matt and Molly were sitting on a pair of swings, gently rocking as Matt listened to Molly read an op-ed from the *Times* about truth telling.

The following shot showed Dr. Diamond walking along University Place while Matt used his hands to shape an idea about patient care. She was clearly impressed with his engaging presentation.

The next clip showed Matt riding on an electric scooter with Molly holding on behind as he zipped along, weaving their way down Wall Street.

Following was a shot taken on a chilly evening showing Molly arm-in-arm with Matt crossing Bowery onto funky Great Jones Street, their heads inclined toward each other while talking quietly. Seemingly without noticing, they passed a vagrant woman bundled in discarded clothing, huddled in a shuttered doorway. Matt slowed to a stop, glanced back at her. He dug out the few coins in his pocket. Molly added a couple dollars and Matt gave it all to the woman, who only nodded vaguely. Then Matt took Molly's arm and they walked on.

The next scene showed Matt almost hit by the Tesla—and the image froze.

Reinhardt scanned back a few frames to hold on Matt and Molly having just helped the homeless woman. Reinhardt studied the image thoughtfully, impressed by their humanism.

Then he picked up his cell and touched the contact number for his employer.

Chapter 2

B y 9:30 the next morning, Reinhardt was riding shotgun in the starboard seat of a blue and white Bell Jet Ranger. The Hudson River was sliding past barely a thousand feet below them. Reinhardt felt his stomach lighten as the pilot began their descent. She was a short-haired female with the assured confidence of a combat veteran. She nodded toward the village they were passing over which was nestled against the river. Her eyes smiled from behind her aviator glasses as she clicked her headset mike and spoke over the engine noise, "Sleepy Hollow. Been up here?"

Reinhardt clicked his mike. "Yep. Had a headless horseman hunt me once." She smiled at his reference to the legendary story. "But I haven't been to where we're going."

"Just a couple miles up." She pointed ahead to what looked like uninhabited park land alongside the river. "I'll give you a quick three-sixty before we set down." She banked the aircraft to cross lower over the railroad tracks that were snug against the shoreline, then she continued over stands of old growth trees on the inland side. "There it is."

In the green countryside ahead, over a mile from the public road, was a large park with broad green lawns and massive stands of two-hundred-year-old trees. Half were deciduous and nearly barren of leaves in November, but an equal number were evergreen, lush and thriving. Sitting in the center of this sixty-seven-acre estate was an imposing mansion built entirely from large, rectangular blocks of granite. Reinhardt's eyes widened as he took it in and the pilot said, "One of the old Vanderbilt places."

It was a Gothic Revival palace that caused Reinhardt to frown curiously. "Hmmm, I've got some *deja vu* going on."

"Like you *have* seen it before? Entirely possible. It's been in a couple movies. I've piloted some aerial camerawork myself a couple of times." Then she added sourly, "before they all started using drones. Actually, my last film gig was here. For that *Downton Abbey* wannabe, *The Gilded Age*."

"Ah. Right." Reinhardt nodded with recognition, "That's exactly where I saw it."

She flew a slow circle around the manor house allowing him to see its impressive mixture of architectural styles. The dominant feature was its square bell tower, twenty feet on the side and rising to six stories above the building's back corner. Halfway up the tower at the fourth story on each side were arched windows ten feet tall and wide with leaded glass. The top floor was an open-air chamber with glassless, fifteen-foot-long colonnaded windows.

He saw that attached to the right of the tower was a substantial three-story wing. On the tower's left, the mansion's main central portion consisted of four large, conjoined buildings of different heights. The tallest had a five-story, steeply pointed roof. There were other Gothic pointed arches of varying sizes everywhere as well as tall, lean, leaded-glass windows.

Reinhardt marveled at it. "Damn thing looks like it *could've* been built in the 13th century."

The pilot brought the helicopter slowly around to fully face the front where a gardener driving a tool-laden golf cart steered to one side to give her space. The pilot settled the chopper gently, gracefully alighting on the front lawn.

Reinhardt saw one of the mansion's two broad, thick front

doors had been opened by an old-school butler who took a few steps out and stood beneath the arched covered portico, awaiting him.

Reinhardt climbed out, retrieving his valise and laptop, then spoke apologetically to the pilot. "I may be a while."

She winked, stifling a yawn. "Take your time, I'm on their dime. I'll just sit out here getting drunk."

Reinhardt smirked, then walked toward the stone arch of the portico. He glanced up at the full front of the granite mansion which loomed imposingly over him as he approached. The clouds above it had darkened, lending a vague uneasiness.

He saw that the trim, balding, white butler watching him approach was perhaps sixty. His eyeglasses had narrow rectangular lenses, suggesting to Reinhardt that he was a man of precision. Neatly dressed in a tailored brown business suit and matching tie with a tan vest beneath his jacket, his attitude was polite, but restrained. Rather than offering his hand, he nodded deferentially saying, "Mr. Reinhardt. Welcome. I am Jamison." He gestured congenially for Reinhardt to enter, and the investigator stepped inside the broad, arched, marble entry foyer where a middle-aged housemaid awaited on the thick oriental carpet beside a beautifully carved, ten-foot coat rack.

She gestured pleasantly toward his raincoat, speaking with an Eastern European accent, "May I, sir?" As she took it, Reinhardt glanced up at the curved arches of the ceiling which were painted to mimic the marble walls. Two life-sized busts of male Romans surmounted pedestals on either side of an inner archway. Just beyond was an oak parquet-floored music and reception room with elegant Georgian furniture, a grand piano and a marble fireplace beneath a huge mirror on its mantle. The nine Greek muses were painted, Renaissance-style, on the sectioned ceiling. Outside light poured in through the three floor-to-ceiling leaded-glass windows that comprised the far wall.

"This way, sir," Jamison said, heading into a side hallway. Reinhardt followed, glancing into large rooms they passed—all with twelve-foot ceilings—including a spacious library two rooms deep, containing plush reading chairs, large globes, a presidential-sized desk, and glass-fronted bookcases fully loaded with countless volumes.

Reinhardt passed a sumptuous dining room with a vaulted, beamed ceiling, walls padded with forest-green cloth wallpaper in between twenty narrow pillars of black marble. The colonnades created nooks containing antique side tables holding marble sculptures and cast bronzes mostly of robust Roman women. All of this surrounded an oak table with twelve padded leather chairs.

During his FBI years Reinhardt had seen a great variety of places, but never any private home so outrageously opulent. Particularly eye-opening was the final Great Hall: even more posh and richly appointed than all preceding and far larger with a lofty thirty-foot Gothic-arched ceiling and a towering three-story window on the far wall.

Reinhardt mumbled, "...Jee-sus!"

"Not an unusual reaction, sir." Jamison sniffed.

Several heavily framed paintings from masters of the Renaissance through Impressionists to early 20th-century surrealists adorned the broad granite walls.

The Great Hall had a few pieces of comfortable 19th- and 20th-century furniture, particularly near the ten-foot fireplace framed by marble pillars supporting a mantle sculpted in early Romantic style.

Reinhardt noted curiously that the expansive chamber was also doing service as a repository and clearing house for historic relics. Sturdy wooden tables along the walls and in the center contained dozens of archaeological finds being scrutinized and sorted by a middle-aged, scholarly-looking couple plus two interns. Many specimens were only fragments, but others were mostly intact, some quite large. Two suits of crusade-era armor stood alongside a table which held various broadswords and a spiked mace with a chain. Another table held a yard-long section of meticulously hand-sewn medieval tapestry protected between Plexiglas sheets. Its illustration was of a victim being tortured by grotesque demons.

Reinhardt passed a table where a child-sized mummy with its wrapping in dusty tatters lay beside a mummified cat with empty eye sockets gaping. Nearby, resting on a cushion of bubble wrap, was an atrophied human forearm, its skin coated with dirt and dried blood, the gritty hand and fingers curled into a claw.

Reinhardt paused, cringing. "Where the hell does he get all this?"

Jamison subtly arched an eyebrow, suggesting, "...Garage sales?"

"Riiiight." Reinhardt smirked, surprised that the staid butler had some humor.

Jamison continued, "Mostly from archeological digs he supervised."

Reinhardt noted boarded-up crates addressed to the Louvre. "And he sells them to museums."

"Correct, sir."

"Looks like they pay pretty well."

The proper butler didn't comment on that, but added, "He's also a historic advisor to several of the majors." As Reinhardt looked again at the clawed hand, Jamison said, "After twenty-two years here, I'm rather used to pieces like these. You find some unsettling?"

Reinhardt nodded. "But also intriguing. He must be an interesting man to work for."

Jamison volunteered nothing, but Reinhardt noticed a shadow cross the man's face, before he said, "The master is upstairs, sir. This way."

As Reinhardt followed toward another Gothic marble archway, he passed a heavy table supporting a gargoyle like those atop Notre

Dame. With its fiendish grin and wide eyes, it appeared to be staring right at him, stone-faced.

Beyond the arch, they climbed a broad mahogany-paneled stairway which had a landing halfway up and a tall window overlooking the grounds and threatening sky. The butler slowed to a stop, pondering, finally speaking in a confidential tone, "If you'll permit me a few private words, sir?"

"Of course," Reinhardt responded, curious.

"Have you ever spoken directly to the master?"

"No, the arrangements were handled through Mr. Deakins, his lawyer. Why, is there a problem?"

"Over the last two months or so, he has been having subtle episodes of what his doctor confides may be oncoming dementia. Or worse."

"Oh, I'm very sorry to hear that," Reinhardt said sincerely. "I went through that with my late mother. Is there memory loss, or—"

"Yes. As well as some sporadic paranoia and even delusion now and again. You may find him quite fine and entirely clear-headed today. Several days in a row often pass where he seems completely normal and then, well, if you've experienced it, you know."

"And I know it requires patience."

"Yes. That's why I thought it best to alert you."

"I appreciate it, Mr. Jamison." Reinhardt extended his hand.

The butler was surprised, but gratified. "Thank you, Mr. Reinhardt." His hand gripped Reinhardt's for a moment. "This way, then."

At the top, Reinhardt was led into a large study with a beamed ceiling and rich wood paneling. He saw that one entire wall had glass-front wooden cabinets containing archeological artifacts.

A gray marble fireplace dominated the inner wall with an oval Baroque mirror overtop. Arranged before it were a red velvet Victorian settee, two matching chairs and a polished tea table. On that table was a sterling silver tray holding an equally sterling tea service.

A leaded-glass window wall was opposite a roll-top desk on one side and a long wooden table on the other. Atop that table, Reinhardt recognized numerous archaeological tools, plus some stone and wooden relics as well as two thick, ancient leather books.

Reinhardt saw a man with his back to them slouching over the table facing a slim, pricy laptop. He had close-cropped, salt-and-pepper hair and appeared to be of mixed White and Black parentage, leaning more toward Black. He wore a light brown country jacket. Even from the back Reinhardt sensed an imposing presence.

Jamison gingerly stepped closer to his master then quietly cleared his throat.

The man's low, gravelly voice grunted, "…Yes?"

"Mr. Reinhardt is here, sir."

"Who's here?" The man's unexpectedly deep bass voice reminded Reinhardt of James Earl Jones. Then he swiveled his chair, and the investigator got his first in-person look at Dr. John Zachery. Reinhardt knew he was eighty, but he looked older. His skin tone was definitely more black than white, with numerous age spots. Reinhardt saw his nose had been broken in his youth. His neatly trimmed full moustache and rounded Van Dyke-style beard matched his hair and eyebrows. He had strong cheekbones which, Reinhardt imagined, if more fleshed out when he was younger, would have lent it fulsomeness. But at his current age his cheeks were sunken, giving him a leaner countenance. His lines and wrinkles were deep.

Reinhardt felt, however, an aura of strong passion and resolute self-will about Zachery. Despite his slouch, he had a commanding, formidable deportment. He tilted his furrowed brow down slightly to peer at the visitor through the vari-focus lenses of his tortoise-shell wireframe glasses. His penetrating gray-green eyes, though slightly bloodshot, suggested keen, literate intelligence. And Reinhardt sensed something more: that subtle self-awareness and myste-riously quiet calm he'd often seen in the eyes of people who possessed a level of power.

But to Reinhardt, Dr. Zachery also seemed a tad confused, eyeing his visitor carefully, trying to make a connection, while sucking some air in through his teeth. "Who?"

"Mis-ter Rein-hardt," the butler carefully articulated, then added supportively, "the gentleman Mr. Deakins engaged to investi-gate your university candidates, sir."

Zachery stared into the distance a moment, processing, finally nodded. "Ah." He beckoned Reinhardt toward the table.

The investigator stepped over, offering his hand. "A pleasure to meet you, Dr. Zachery."

Zachery shook his hand distractedly, mumbling a greeting, then he noticed the butler waiting attentively and said, "Thank you... uh..."

The manservant patiently prompted, "Jamison, sir."

"Of course." Zachery seemed slightly embarrassed. "... Jamison."

The butler shared a private glance with Reinhardt, which rein-forced their preceding conversation. Then Jamison picked up an empty crystal glass nearby. "More pear juice, sir?" Zachery shook his head absently. "Will that be all then, sir?"

"Yes, thank you...Jamison." The butler nodded respectfully, watching his master's gaze drift downward as the old man sighed wistfully. Jamison shared a last glance with Reinhardt and exited.

But the moment the door closed, Reinhardt noticed Zachery's eyes slowly rise to look steadily, carefully at the door, as if to be certain the butler had truly walked away. A moment of paranoia, perhaps? Then Zachery inhaled and his cloudiness seemed to evapo-rate. He rose from his chair, beckoning congenially, "Here, Mr. Reinhardt, I'll make some space for you." He began moving the items on his worktable.

Seeing the older man standing and less slouched, Reinhardt assessed his aging physique. His shoulders might have been much broader in his younger years, but now were slightly hunched, shortening his height to slightly below six feet. His pants seemed baggy, indicating how younger hips and legs had been reduced in size and strength. Otherwise, he seemed fairly fit for eighty. He carefully slid aside the two books, each about twenty inches square and thick as an unabridged dictionary. Their heavy leather covers were cracked and ancient, the paper inside yellowed, rough-edged.

"They've been around a while." Reinhardt said while taking the four files from his laptop case.

"Late eleventh century," Zachery confirmed, raising his eyebrows for emphasis. "One of them supposedly contains the Philosopher's Stone."

"The what?"

"The legendary Philosopher's Stone was the illusive formula for turning base metals into gold. One of many magical transformations sought by ancient alchemists. Including Sir Isaac Newton."

"Really? The physicist, mathematician?"

"Plus theologian, astronomer, author, philosopher, and sometimes thoroughly deranged genius. Newton evolved into all of those after his disappointing efforts at alchemy."

Reinhardt opened his laptop. "Have *you* had any luck, doc?"

"Quite a bit overall, yes," Zachery said with a wry smile, "but not as yet in that area of alchemy. Like so much of antiquity, that answer remains elusive." He resumed his chair, indicating a nearby stool for his visitor.

Then Zachery glanced at the covers of the four folders, each bearing a photo of the student documented. "Are they arranged in any particular order?"

"Just alphabetical, sir." Reinhardt booted his laptop. "And I also have video material of each as you'd requested."

"Very well," Zachery said pleasantly, "let's have a look at these young folks." He opened the Z-1 folder, which contained a half dozen pages, and peered down through his tortoiseshell wireframes.

It took an hour for Zachery to read carefully through the first three reports, often pulling his lower lip thoughtfully. He asked Reinhardt questions and encouraged the investigator's personal comments on each candidate while watching their individual surveillance videos. As he closed the third folder he said, "Well. Three excellent candidates." Then he opened Matt's dossier, glanced over it briefly, saying, "Run the next video and remind me about this one."

"Matthew William Shaw, second-year med school," Reinhardt said as his laptop began displaying the surveillance videos of Matt going about daily concerns. "Three-point-eight-five GPA. Very diligent. His professors and other TAs are unanimously positive, as you'll see in their recommendation letters and our interview summaries. He's modest, self-effacing, and trusted by his fellow students, though he doesn't seek the limelight. Paying his own way through school, he's been employed for a year nearly full time at Med-X Laboratories which confirms his excellent worth ethic. He is also a computer whiz and helps with their IT issues. Very little savings. Owes some hefty college loans."

Zachery glanced from the video to look for something in the dossier. "Family?"

"None living. Parents were anthropologists and—"

"Oh yes, yes." Zachery noted a reference in the report. "I remember now. I actually knew his parents slightly." He saw another notation, frowned. "His father was killed in a hit-and-run?"

"Just before Matthew was born, yes. His mother died of cancer when he was eighteen. He's very health conscious. Non-smoker. Only an occasional beer with his chicken-tomato-basil pizza. No drug use. Chews a lot of Tums. Likable. Generous."

Zachery's gray-green eyes studied Reinhardt cagily. "You're partial to this one."

Reinhardt shrugged. "Seems like a particularly nice, deserving kid."

As Zachery watched the videos of Matt, he opened a bottle of yellow prescription pills, took one with a sip of water from a cut-crystal glass as a new video image included Dev.

"His roommate, Dev Bhandari," Reinhardt described, "Mumbai native. Pre-med. Good student. Little on the retro-fringy side. It's all in the file. Also, a work-up on her, too."

Molly had appeared. Zachery was struck by her sunny face and auburn hair. "My, my. His lady fair?"

"For seven months. Molly Perez. They are very devoted."

The older man assessed her lovely face, confidently surmising, "A Tisch theater student, no doubt."

"No, sir. History and Journalism. Double major. First-year graduate."

"Surprising. Given those looks."

Reinhardt saw Zachery's appreciation of Molly. He felt it was the classic image of a man in the winter of his life recalling the springtime.

After a few more scenes another came up that particularly caught Zachery's attention. The video was of Matt seen from behind, jogging at a good pace along the East River Promenade. It had been recorded in warmer September weather. He was shirtless, in only shorts and sneakers. His physique was muscular. He was being photographed unaware by a GoPro camera mounted on the front of a bicycle that tracked him from behind. Then the camera glided past him, and the image switched to a rear-facing GoPro point of view revealing the graceful Williamsburg Bridge behind him. Matt continued running while enjoying his view of Brooklyn on the far side. A couple of women he passed enjoyed their view of his well-honed six pack and strong legs.

Zachery pulled thoughtfully at his lower lip as he watched

Matt. Reinhardt thought it was somewhat like watching an expert stable owner assessing a thoroughbred's possibilities.

When the montage video ended, Zachery inhaled deeply. He laid down Matt's dossier atop the others and said with finality, "Well done, Mr." —he paused to recall— "...Reinhardt."

The investigator was stowing his laptop. "Thank you, Dr. Zachery. I'm glad you're pleased. And this thumb drive contains all the files and videos."

Zachery took and inserted it into his own laptop. "Always like to confirm that components function properly." He was gratified to see a main menu appear with the four candidates' names and photos. A click on Matthew's accessed a submenu with icons for text and video. He started the surveillance footage; let it play for a few seconds and paused it. "Very well. I think we're squared away..."

Then Zachery stood—flinching slightly and grunting with annoyance. "Ouch. Sitting too damn long." He went to his rolltop desk where he picked up a business envelope. Reinhardt stood up respectfully as Zachery walked back. The doctor took another deep breath and twisted slightly as though to unkink his back. "You and your associates did six months' worth of research in only three." His arthritic hand offered the envelope. "And I've decided to reward you accordingly."

Reinhardt was surprised and received it with his head graciously inclined. "Well. That's...very generous of you, Dr. Zachery."

"You've earned it." The doctor nodded formally and turned away to sit down facing his laptop. "Good day."

Being a former Marine, Reinhardt recognized that he'd been dismissed, but said, "If you need anything further—"

"I shan't." Zachery restarted the video, intent on watching it, saying conclusively, "You can find your way out, I'm sure."

"Certainly, sir. And thanks again for—"

"My pleasure," Zachery mumbled without looking back. Meeting over.

Okay. Well then. Reinhardt thought.

He walked across the study, opened the door then took a last look around the room with its peculiar artifacts and back at the doctor, who was facing away. Reinhardt knew instinctively that Zachery had already forgotten about him. He was busy scanning the video of Matthew Shaw. Reinhardt saw him pause the images momentarily on Matt's face, then on Molly's, then Zachery let play the scene of Matt running shirtless on the East River Promenade.

Finally, Reinhardt stepped into the hall, pulling the door almost closed. But not quite. He hesitated, pondering the curious old man, and feeling an unusual frustration that he would likely never know the inside story of what happened next—particularly to the young people into whose lives he'd had a momentary, tantalizing glimpse. He felt a fleeting ache of disappointment.

But then his professionalism caught up. He drew a breath, and quietly closed the door.

Chapter 3

Matt and Molly had often paused on LaGuardia Place in the Village to admire the beauty of the One World Trade Center tower which stood majestically above lower Manhattan. But that crystal-clear night they were hustling quickly around the intersection at West Third Street and into the NYU Alumni Building.

Moments later they emerged from the elevator at the penthouse as Molly asked, "You ever been up here before?"

"No," Matt said, feeling intimidated. "And I wish I wasn't now." He was embarrassed being dressed in jeans and his skimpy jacket.

"Hey." She responded supportively. "You're a hard-working student who got stuck at his job and—"

"Yeah, but I couldn't get to that four o'clock m-meeting they also wanted me at."

"Dr. Diamond told you not to worry about—"

"But she's not dressed like I am or—" He saw something ahead. Went pale. "Oh shit."

They were approaching the wide, polished walnut entrance doors to a beautifully appointed gathering room with four crystal chandeliers hanging from the high ceiling. Forty or so nicely dressed men and women of varying ethnicities and ages were chatting, sipping drinks, selecting canapés from a passing waiter. The attendees included some faculty whom Matt and Molly recognized, plus a few grad students. The rest were graying, or trying-not-to-be-graying alumni.

"Come on, let's boldly go." Molly took his arm, determined to wade in successfully, though Matt steered them closer to the wall.

Matt saw that the room consisted of eight or nine areas where comfortable chairs or love seats faced each other around cocktail tables inviting smaller groups for conversations. But the room was spacious enough to allow for mingling and stand-up encounters.

Molly was eyeing people investigatively. She was very comfortable.

Matt was very *un.* "I have no idea why I was invited or wh-what I'm supposed to be doing here."

"I'm certain all will be revealed, Matty. Meanwhile check out these fascinating people." Her bright, sharp eyes were darting from one to another.

Matt noticed a couple of them were glancing at him with peculiar, enigmatic smiles. He whispered to Molly, "Some are looking at me weirdly."

"Give it right back to them. I always try to make a game out of it. See what I can deduce about people."

"C'mon, Moll. The surface look isn't—"

"Oh, I know: 'can't always judge a book by its cover,' but—"

"That's good. My binding's pretty ragged." He embarrassedly showed her the frayed cuff of his shirt, then pulled down his thin windbreaker sleeve to hide it.

"But you *can* pick up clues," she continued, "about what's going on inside by what's outside." She gestured subtly toward a distinguished older man. "Like Dean Sanger over there. He's stubborn, vain and doesn't want to admit he's getting older."

Matt looked at the college dean, William Sanger, who appeared about seventy and was engaged in a conversation with an attractive young grad school TA while trying to read a business card at arm's length.

"Okay," Matt acknowledged, "obviously 'getting older' because he has to hold that card out to read it."

"Right."

"But 'stubborn and vain'?"

Molly gave Matt a challenging glance of *figure it out, Bozo*. He puffed with annoyance, but studied the dean more carefully, then smiled wryly. "Ah. Stubborn. Because the glasses he obviously needs to use are right there in his coat pocket, but he refuses to use 'em."

Molly nodded. "And vain because…"

"He doesn't want the hottie TA to know he needs them."

"See?" Molly kissed his cheek. "Way to go, Sherlock!"

Matt chuckled, calmed a bit.

Dean Sanger glanced around the room and his eyes caught on them. His face lit up with a smile. He approached, extending his hand. "Matthew, good to see you, son."

"You, too, sir." Matt shook the dean's hand, apologetic. "I'm so s-sorry I couldn't be at that four o'clock meeting, I was working at Med-X, didn't even have time to change before—"

"No worries," Sanger said, waving it away. "Pauline called. Said she'd held you hostage giving CPR to her lab computers." His eyes turned to Molly, squinting slightly, trying to place her. "And… Mary, isn't it? No, it's—"

"Very close. Molly. Perez." She shook his hand. Firmly.

"Forgive me, Molly. And you're in Carter, right? Grad in History?"

"And Journalism. Yes."

"Ah! A double threat."

Matt noticed the dean seemed as eager to impress Molly as he had the TA. Sanger leaned slightly closer to her saying, "Sorry I can't know all the students in my own department as well—or as long—as I've known this guy." He put an arm around Matt's shoulder, speaking sincerely. "We're very proud of you, Matt. And as a matter of fact, that's why you're here." He raised his eyebrows for emphasis. "The important alumnus from that afternoon meeting is here tonight." With a touch of the dramatic he beckoned, "Walk this way…"

The dean guided them through the crowded room toward the far side where laughter was emanating from. Matt saw a slouching gentleman who stood facing away from them while conversing with a delighted group of faculty alumni and several grad students. One grad was a pale redhead, and another guy was black with dreads pulled back tightly and fastened into a ponytail. They, along with the others, were facing the gentleman like starstruck fans, feeling amazed to be chatting with him.

Molly's eyes suddenly popped wide. She muttered, "Oh my God!"

Matt was startled; whispered, "What?"

He saw she was transfixed, sensed that her heart was pounding. Her voice became a quavering whisper of wonderment as they got closer. "Oh my God. It *is* him!"

"Him who?" Matt was puzzled.

Dean Sanger called out to the man, "Excuse me?"

The gentleman turned to look at them. His wrinkled, mixed-race face warmed with a captivating smile.

Matt remained bewildered and saw that Molly was about to wet her pants.

Sanger made introductions. "John, this is the med student who couldn't be with us this afternoon, Matthew Shaw. And Molly Perez, history-journalism masters." Then Sanger looked at the two of them. "Matt and Molly, meet the one-and-only Dr. John—"

"Zachery." Molly blurted, barely not gushing. "Of course!"

Behind his glasses, Zachery's gray-green eyes lighted with pleasure as he took her lovely hand. His manner was easy, cordial, showing perfect but unobtrusive confidence in himself.

Molly's mouth was dry. "It's a very great honor, Doctor—"

"John, please," he said in his stirring *basso profundo* voice. "And you're a history major? Well done."

"Thanks," Molly beamed. "But at this moment I feel more like an *astronomy* major meeting Neil de Grasse Tyson."

"I definitely take that as a compliment." He winked with warmth, still holding her hand for emphasis. "And Neil's a good friend, so I'll pass it along."

Matt was trying to piece together why Zachery looked vaguely familiar, with his close-cropped African-heritage hair sprinkled as though with powdered sugar, his face and features slightly more Black than Anglo and that signature Van Dyke-style moustache and beard matching his hair.

"And hello Matthew—" Zachery shook Matt's hand heartily. "—who is very lucky indeed to have such a charming lady by his side."

"You're r-right about that, sir. It's a pleasure to meet you."

"Well, *I* had the pleasure of knowing your parents, my boy. Met your mother briefly on a Smithsonian dig in—where was it," he pulled on his lower lip, straining to remember, "perhaps Tunisia, if memory serves." He chuckled, trading a glance with longtime colleague Sanger, as he confessed, "Which memory does less and less accurately these days."

"Now, stop saying that, John," Sanger chided supportively, "you're doing fine memory-wise."

"I wish." Then Zachery looked back at Matt. "I think your father and I later had a friendly rivalry over some antiquity or other."

"Before my time, I'm afraid," Matt said.

"Indeed, it was before you were born." Then Zachery spoke more gently, "I'm very sorry that the world lost them both. And far too young."

Dean Sanger agreed sadly, "Two of my dearest friends."

"And their contributions to cultural anthropology," Zachery added, "were extraordinary."

Matt nodded. "Thanks, I've always thought so."

"*Your* contributions certainly have been, too, Doctor," Molly eagerly interjected. "Your *Ted Talk* last month comparing English and American History was startling. Like your whole PBS series. The way you talk—and write—about the past always makes me feel like I was right there."

"Very kind of you, Molly," Zachery said modestly, lowering his voice to share a secret, "but it's a simple trick—'*Satis vivat et tu pars historiae fies.*'"

Matt took a crack at translating the Latin. "'Live long enough…you become part of history?'"

"Precisely, Matthew!" Zachery laughed appreciatively, triggering a small cough.

"Hey, speak for yourself, John," Sanger chided, then winked to Matt and Molly, "He's actually a *lot* older than me."

Zachery countered good naturedly, "In your dreams, Willy."

They all laughed. Molly shot Matt a private glance that said *I told you Sanger didn't want to admit aging.*

Then Zachery focused on Matt. "Might I possibly steal you away from this striking young journalist-historian for a few minutes, Matthew?"

Matt blinked. "Uh…" He glanced toward Molly who nodded, urging him and Dean Sanger—who had a peculiar smile and raised his graying eyebrows with definite encouragement. Then Matt looked quizzically at Zachery, nodding. "Of c-course, sir."

Zachery turned to acknowledge his eager groupies nearby, saying graciously, "It's been wonderful conversing with you all. I appreciate you tolerating my crumbling memory." They all expressed gratitude, and several applauded politely.

Matt noticed that the redhead, the dread-head, and a brunette female student, who might have been Iranian or Arabic, all seemed to be smiling strangely at him just as Sanger had.

Turning to leave with the doctor, Matt's eyes locked onto Molly's, and they shared a private nanosecond of curiosity: *What's going on?*

~~~~

MATT WALKED WITH DR. ZACHERY OUT THROUGH THE impressive, two-story, sculptured archway of the Alumni Building's main entrance onto the Third Street sidewalk. The older man had donned an overcoat. Two blue-and-white NYU flags wafted overhead in the chill November breeze, which Zachery inhaled deeply then coughed slightly and tapped his sternum. "Sorry. Fighting a little chest thing. This cold air is better. But are you warm enough, son? That jacket looks terribly thin."

"I'm fine, sir. Thanks."

Zachery pulled out a cigar which he unwrapped as they walked westward toward LaGuardia Place. There was little traffic and only a few people about. Zachery lit the stogie and puffed, enjoying the taste. "My doctor tells me I shouldn't, of course, but as Eric the Red once said, '*Hva faen har jeg a tape.*'"

Matt smiled. "With Latin I have a chance, Dr. Zachery. But not with—was it Swedish?"

"Norwegian. Roughly translates as 'what the hell have I got to lose.' I'd offer you one of these Havanas, Matthew, but you don't smoke."

"No, I… That's right, sir." He frowned with curiosity.

The old guy seemed to be enjoying Matt's confusion. "I'll try to stay downwind."

"Thanks." Matt walked quietly, biding his time.

After a few steps Zachery sucked some air between his teeth. "So. Still planning to specialize in oncology research?"

Matt remained patient, trying to suss out what was going on. "Yes, sir."

"Because of your mother's stomach cancer?"

Matt blinked. That was pretty close to home. "Partly, y-yes. Excuse me, but—"

"Oh, I've had my eye on you, Matthew. And three other students recommended to me by Willy and the deans." He chuckled. "Sounds like a 50s rock group."

Matt was amused. "It does."

"I met with the other three this afternoon. They were also up there tonight."

Matt added it up. "The guy with dreads, the redhead and a female brunette?"

Correct," he said approvingly. "Very observant."

Matt was thinking, *Okay, and...?*

"The deans all tell me you're the hardest working of the lot."

Matt shrugged. "Don't know about that, sir. Just trying to get through."

"They also say you're too modest, son." He pointed with his cigar. "You're exceptional, Matthew. You'd have to be," he grinned, "to enjoy the company of the obviously bright and engaging Ms. Perez."

Matt glanced at the older man, whose sharp eyes held steady on Matt. "Yes, sir. Molly's a gem. Best thing that ever happened to me."

"I'm delighted to hear that." Zachery steered them onto Thompson Street. As they walked a vista opened up: in the distant uptown skyline the Empire State Building could be seen. But dominating the scene just in front of them was Washington Square Park with its triumphal, seventy-three-foot white marble arch standing out brightly in the night. Zachery inhaled. "I always love this view. You know why the arch was built back in 1891?"

"To honor George Washington?" Matt surmised politely, trying to remain patient.

"Actually, to commemorate his inauguration as President a century earlier." The historian's gaze became a bit distant. "Those late-1700s were a *very* interesting time indeed."

Matt nodded agreement, but remained silent, looking straight ahead as they walked.

"Okay." Zachery finally smiled. "I know I'm exhausting your patience but chalk it up to one of the few pleasures an old man has left: stretching out the enjoyment of being the bearer of glad tidings. If Ms. Perez is the best thing that ever happened to you, Matthew—and from meeting her I think you're correct—then I hope to be the *second*-best thing." He drew a breath and continued, his voice sounding even deeper. "Here's the deal, son: I've been fortunate. Managed to put some money by. But I have no family, no heirs. So, I've decided to endow full scholarships for four worthy students. Including you."

Matt stopped, astonished. "Wh-what?"

Zachery clearly enjoyed Matt's amazement as they stood facing each other on the sidewalk of Washington Square South. "I'll also wipe out your student loans, set up the money you need for med school and beyond, through any post-doctoral studies."

Matt stared.

"And I'll arrange enough extra to get you and the other three some excellent healthcare coverage plus moderate living expenses."

"No, no." Matt waved negatively. "Dr. Zachery, th-that's too much!"

"Well, I did say *moderate*."

"No, listen...sir," Matt sputtered, "I've g-got a good job. I can keep working—"

"Better to be one hundred percent focused on your education."

"But you're talking about..." his addled brain did flip-flops adding it up, "about a half-million d-dollars' worth of schooling!"

"Really?" the old man frowned. "Would it be *that* much?—Well then, forget it."

Matt blinked.

Zachery grinned, met his eyes, on the level. "Matthew, it will be my pleasure."

Matt was overwhelmed. "But I...I...don't know what to s-say. I..."

Zachery rested a hand on Matt's shoulder. "When I was your age and this same offer was made to me, I didn't know either." They resumed walking slowly toward the winter-dry fountain in the center of the square. An expression of fond memory crossed Zachery's craggy face. "My benefactor was Alberto Costanza. He'd amassed a considerable fortune in the 1930s during Prohibition. Rascal had been an 'alcohol importer.' Polite words for 'rumrunner.' In later years he frequented the gym in Queens where in the mid-60s I was an eighteen-year-old training as a boxer."

Matt was astounded. "A boxer?"

"Yes. Sixty-five pounds heavier then and all muscle. Local coach thought I had some promise, a chance to make a living. Mr. Costanza took an interest, but a few weeks later he learned about my real passion."

"Which was...?"

"History. I was never the greatest student, but I loved history. The lessons it teaches. Turned out Mr. C was a history buff, too. One day after a local match I was taking off my gloves and wiping away some blood from my eyes and broken nose, and he said, 'Listen kid, why don't you take them gloves off *forever*?' I told him I needed the dough, and he came back with, 'Well what if you *didn't*?'" Zachery slowed to a stop. "His offer was like mine to you. He made me flush. Also got me a shot at Harvard and—"

"But, I mean, wh-what can I possibly do in return to—?"

"Exactly what I asked Mr. C. And he said, 'Study up, kid, then go fulfill your fondest dream. Make this world a better place.' For me that meant growing my love for history, spreading that knowledge so folks might reap some benefit."

His aged, gray-green eyes gazed deeply into Matt's youthful blue eyes for an extended moment. Then he smiled. Wistfully, it seemed to Matt. Dr. Zachery took a final puff on his cigar, then studied it, pondering. "In your case, Matthew," he paused to crush out the unfinished cigar on a trash can and drop it in. "In your case, I'd probably suggest: how about you go find a cure for cancer?"

Matt felt the full weight of that profound challenge. Then inhaled deeply. "That is my goal, sir. I will surely do my best."

Zachery held out his hand, which Matt clasped. "I'm confident you will, son. And have a happy, worthwhile life doing it." Then another pleasant thought occurred to the old man. "And you know, there is one other little thing…"

Matt glanced warily. Was there a catch? He was hesitant to ask. "Which is…?"

"Someday, when you're much older—and successful—remember to 'pay it forward,' help out a few deserving students."

Matt laughed. "*That* is something you can absolutely count on."

They shared a long look, then Matt glanced up toward the square's arch looming above them. A light, feathery snowfall had begun. An image and a moment he would always remember.

As they walked quietly back the way they had come, Matt's head was spinning in several dimensions at once. Passing a small chapel on the park's periphery that contained a weathered statue of a saint, Matt caught a glimpse of its marble face, its unblinking eyes looking straight at him, having borne witness to the scene.

Chapter 4

An hour after his walk with Dr. Zachery, Matt, Molly, and Dev burst happily into the 1920s four-floor walk-up the guys shared at Bleeker and Bank in Greenwich Village. It had typical poor-student touches: makeshift bookshelves with old boards held up by used bricks; a scratched-up door served as a worktable/desk for their laptops. Dev dumped his coat on his rickety desk chair. His end of the table featured geek-worthy collectibles including his carefully wrapped classic comic book collection, a *Dr. Who* mailbox, a baby Yoda, a bobblehead of Thelma Greer, a reptilian action figure from the old *V* miniseries, a stretchable Hulk doll, etc. Also vintage was his touch-tone telephone and digital answering machine.

Dev was effusive but wary. "I still simply cannot believe it!"

"*You* can't." Matt was humbled, his brain swirling as he gazed at the *Gray's Anatomy* posters he'd memorized of human circulatory and nervous systems on the wall over his section of worktable. Molly dusted snow from his jacket as he took it off.

"There is some hidden agenda," Dev said with narrowed eyes while walking in a slow circle around the small, battered coffee table in front of their worn, brown corduroy couch, his overactive mind churning. "It reeks of conspiracy."

Matt also pondered as he picked up a Tums pack from atop the dented, two-drawer file cabinet serving as an end table to the couch. "Seems too good to be true, huh?"

Dev nodded. "As we say in my country, 'fucking A, bubba.'"

"You guys are both full of shit." Molly hugged Matt. "Dr. Zachery couldn't pick a better person."

"Sure, he could!" Dev blurted emphatically. "Me!"

"But Dev," Molly explained gently, hanging her puffy coat on one of their mismatched chairs, "he clearly wanted people from Earth." She pointed to the poster over Dev's desk—a spiral galaxy with a YOU ARE HERE arrow pointing at our sun. A Post-it note in the darkness outside the galaxy bore Matt's handwritten message DEV IS OVER HERE!

Dev dismissed her theory but caught a glimpse of himself in their small wall mirror, eyeing his hair that was swept up into its tall, crownlike pile. "Maybe if I'd brushed it down, he'd have picked me."

Matt felt awkward. "I don't know what to say, Dev... I'm s-sorry. Really."

Dev turned to stare at his roommate blankly. "You are amazing." He glanced at Molly. "He is amazing."

She thoroughly agreed. "No kidding."

Matt was confused. "Why?"

She smiled. "Apologizing for your own good luck, Matty."

"Yes!" Dev shouted. "A *normal* struggling med student with a mountain of debt living in this dive with a threadbare faux Persian rug would be whooping it up. Or inflating his ego—"

"Bigger than Buzz Lightyear at the Macy's Parade," Molly confirmed.

Matt shook his head. "I just can't stop wondering: why m-me?"

Dev arched his eyebrows, taking on a serious but twinkling expression, and did an excellent Rod Serling impression: "Presented for your approval: Matthew Shaw, a perplexed young medical student who has just stepped out of poverty and into... *The Scholarship Zone.*"

"There's no mystery, Matt." Molly was certain. "Zachery picked the right guy. And sooo—did I." She drew Matt toward his bedroom, which was almost large enough to turn around in if the futon was rolled up.

Dev raised a forefinger. "But you should be remembering, Mr. Shaw, how you promised me ten percent of any newfound wealth."

Matt inclined his head favorably. "You shall not be forgotten, Mr. Bhandari."

Molly smiled back at Dev as she closed the bedroom door. "Will you excuse us, sir?"

"Oh yes, yes, by all means," Dev grumbled, looking around, "I will just be out here with the sharp-pointed objects."

~~~~

MOMENTS LATER, MATT AND MOLLY, UNCLOTHED, SETTLED onto his futon. She gave him a long, congratulatory kiss, but sensed his distraction and understood. "Not quite in the moment?" Matt shook his head. "Gee, why not? After such a boring, *uneventful* evening."

She lovingly stroked the lock of sandy-brown hair on his forehead. "When you left, Dean Sanger insisted I have a drink with him. He told me how Dr. Zachery narrowed his candidates to you four. Even had a private eye watching you all. Shooting video."

Matt frowned. "That's creepy."

"Not the way it turned out," Molly reminded. "I knew some of Zachery's 'Heavyweight-to-Harvard' story, but Sanger told me about the Costanza guy—who *had* been a Capone type that dodged prison—but only a few days after endowing Zachery, Costanza was killed by a mob hit!"

"Are you serious!?"

"Dead serious." Then Molly grimaced. "I can't believe I said that. Anyway, Costanza *also* left young Zachery a Hudson River mansion plus his *whole fortune!* Zachery dazzled Harvard with his encyclopedic knowledge of history, then earned his NYU doctorate crazy-fast. He's got a savant-level memory for details that audiences —like me—love hearing him talk about."

"Yeah. All impressive for sure, but..." Matt's face crinkled, bewildered.

Molly nuzzled him. "What's eating you, Matty? On such a triumphant night?"

"I think that's exactly it, Moll: tonight *wasn't* a triumph for me. It was a *gift.*" She started to object—but he anticipated her. "Yes, an incredible gift. But something I'd *deserved?* I mean, yes, I'm thrilled. But you know I've always worried if I can become a really good oncologist and this gigantic, f-free gift adds a huge responsibility. Adds an extra ton of weight to—"

"To *what!*" She laughed as she leapt right on top of him, pretending to throttle his neck. "Adds weight to *what?* Tell me!" She shook him playfully. "I know you *know*, so say it! 'Adds weight to your—'?"

"Okay," he was laughing. "To what you call my '*Imposter Syndrome*'!"

"Not just what *I* call it." Molly leaned nose-to-nose; her auburn mane hung down, creating a hair tent over their faces. "It's what everyone who knows you will verify!"

He tickled her sides and she yelped, releasing his neck. "Nooooo! Tickling not fair!"

She landed alongside him, still laughing. "Oh, Matty," she breathed a frustrated sigh. "If only you believed in yourself as much as we all do. Dr. Zachery certainly knows you're special."

Matt rose on an elbow facing her uncertainly. "I'll try, okay?" Then he leaned closer and kissed her lovingly, finally getting into the moment.

Molly whispered, "I am so happy for you."

"Mmm. Me, too," he purred back, in between small kisses, "Particularly right…now."

His fingers caressed her silky skin. His lips lightly kissed their way down her slender side and grazed over the small, heart-shaped beauty mark on her hip. Molly smiled with tranquil pleasure. His fingertips massaged her gently. They were comfortable together. Their lovemaking was tender. And easy.

~~~~

THE NEXT MORNING AT TEN-THIRTY MATT WAS WEARING HIS only sport jacket, a dark navy blazer, over the sky-blue shirt that Molly said set off his eyes. His only dress pants were dark gray, his sneakers black. He was standing beside the dreadlocked candidate who wore an inexpensive dark suit and black turtleneck. They were facing the floor-to-ceiling glass window thirty-eight stories above Sixth Avenue gazing at vast Manhattan spreading below them from midtown to Central Park and beyond. The other student muttered in amazement, "Can you believe this whole thing?"

Matt's response was barely audible. "…No."

A solid oak door opened in the high-end lobby containing an understated, stylish sign, LAGUARDIA & DEAKINS, LEGAL. A lean, natty, middle-aged attorney with a thousand-dollar hairpiece ushered out the redheaded student, handing him a thick legal file envelope, saying, "Your new JPMorgan Chase card is in there and Dr. Bleifer is expecting you at the NYU Health Center for your insurance physical. Congratulations again." The redhead thanked him as they shook hands, then turned to stare wide-eyed at his two comrades and silently mouthed an exuberant, *Wow!*

The lawyer smiled at Matt. "Matthew Shaw?"

"Y-yes sir."

He eyed Matt with particular interest, extending his hand. "Gary Deakins. John's attorney. Come on back, we'll get you squared away." Then to the dreadlocked guy and the seated brunette female he said, "Just be a few minutes and you'll all be on your way."

~~~~

THREE HOURS LATER MATT WAS BACK IN STUDENT GARB AS Dev hurried to keep pace with him crossing busy University Place near the Med-X lab. It was freezing. Steam rose from manhole covers. Dev spoke with concern, "No, really, Mattsy, I have been analyzing this from multiple perspectives. It is much too good to be true."

"T-tell me about it," Matt said shaking his head. "I keep waiting to wake up."

"I am just warning you, man: if they do a rectal probe—"

"It's 'definitely an alien conspiracy.' Got it." Matt peeled off, heading into the health center.

Dev yelled after him, "I'm serious!"

"I know. That's what scares me," Matt shouted back, laughing. "Too many Thelma Greer conventions!"

In an examining room Matt wore an open-back exam gown, talking through his uneventful medical history while a Filipino nurse practitioner typed details into their system. He reported no meds, except occasional Tums for a grumbly stomach. Matt left urine and the nurse drew blood. He also took a peculiar breath test to check gases in his system.

Dr. Elise Bleifer, a friendly-faced, fortyish woman introduced herself and proceeded through an extensive physical. Just when Matt thought she'd finished, she explained how the insurance company required an EKG treadmill stress test which she'd set up for him nearby. "Lastly," she added apologetically as she pulled on a blue Nitrile glove, "they also require a digital exam."

As Matt bent forward over the table and the doctor inserted her finger, probing to check his prostate, he laughed to himself about confirming to Dev that it *was* an alien abduction.

After he completed the treadmill test, he was told that Dr. Bleifer would ring him with the test results tomorrow.

～～～～

THAT CALL CAME IN AS MATT WAS EXITING HIS SYSTEMATIC Pathology classroom, about to head to Med-X for a few hours of work. A cheerful Dr. Bleifer reported, "You sailed through everything, Matthew. That breath test indicated the presence of some excess hydrogen gas suggesting your grumbling innards have SIBO, Small Intestine Bacterial Overgrowth. I know that sounds sort of gross, but it's zero to worry about. A mild antibiotic will smooth you out. We've sent the results to the insurance company. I'm sure they'll think you're good to go. Congratulations!"

An hour later at Med-X, Matt had successfully rebooted a troublesome computer, caught up with a stack of pathology reports, and finally opened his own laptop to do Behavioral Science homework when Dean William Sanger called offering more salutations for Matt's good fortune. "And Dr. Zachery is hoping you might give him the pleasure of your company for dinner tomorrow night. Is that a possibility?"

"Absolutely, sir!"

Then Sanger spoke more quietly. "There is some bad news, I'm afraid."

Matt tightened up. "S-sir?"

Sanger almost whispered, "They require gentlemen to wear a tie."

"Oh," Matt tried to match Sanger's low-key, faux seriousness, "W-well, in that case, sir, I'll have to pass."

The dean laughed. "Well spoken, lad! We'll text you the details. And give the old bastard my regards." He added fondly, "Enjoy your dinner, Matthew. And your upcoming life."

Matt thanked Dean Sanger sincerely as they said goodbye. Then Matt sat, mulling it

all. He was still afraid to acknowledge the bubble of joy in his chest.

Chapter 5

M att was amazed by what could be seen through the expansive windows of Moonshadows. It was a watering hole of the well-to-do atop Liberty Court, a mostly residential building just off Battery Place in lower Manhattan. He saw stunning views southward across the harbor, from Ellis Island and Lady Liberty to the spectacular Verrazzano-Narrows suspension bridge. To the north, the Trade Center complex and its 1,776-foot-tall tower seemed close enough to touch.

The restaurant interior was elegantly understated, but nonetheless clearly expressed elite taste and pricey entrees.

With impeccable finesse, a highly tipped sommelier topped off Matt's champagne glass with a bit more Dom. Being almost a teetotaler, Matt had been barely sipping to be polite, but he already felt a buzz.

He glanced at the posh clientele, mostly older but with encouraging diversity. A cocktail pianist in black tie played softly. Dr. Zachery had allowed their conversation to be interrupted by a ravishing, thirty-something woman. She'd apologized profusely, asking for his autograph which he was providing graciously. "There you go, Ms. Wilkins."

Matt saw how much she enjoyed hearing her name spoken by Zachery's sonorous bass voice. She blushed, nodded thanks, and retreated. Zachery coughed slightly, taking a yellow prescription pill as Matt watched the woman proudly show the autograph to a friend. "I wonder how many historians get asked to sign cocktail napkins?"

Zachery shrugged it off. "It's only because of the PBS series." He lifted his champagne flute toward Matt, "She should be toasting you, my boy."

Matt clinked his glass, then took another baby sip. "I swear Dr. Zachery, if I have another glass—"

"Then I might get you to call me John?"

"It seems disrespectful. But if you insist," he raised his glass, "to you...John."

Zachery smiled and his many wrinkles seemed to double in number. "To us, Matthew."

Their glasses clinked. "Did you buy this much champagne for the other three at their lunch today?"

"No, but you're the last." Zachery cleared his throat. "And if I imbibe enough, I might finally shake this damn cold."

"Can I ask why I got a solo dinner?"

"You and I have a special connection, Matthew."

"Because you'd met my parents?"

"Precisely. Did you accompany your mother on any digs?"

"Africa twice. Met the Leaky family at Olduvai Gorge."

"Marvelous."

"And in Peru when Mom's team found—"

"That ancient man frozen in the Andes?" Zachery's eyes brightened. "Must have been remarkable."

"Big time." Matt spoke confidentially. "I wasn't supposed to, but I just had to touch him."

"Ah." Zachery was enthused. "Don't you love that! Even after all these years, I'm always excited by a new artifact. It's as though you're actually touching the past."

Matt slurred slightly, "That's exshactly—sorry, my lips are numb —ex-act-ly what my mother used to say."

"Oh. That reminds me, something I wanted to show you." He patted his coat pockets. "If I remembered to bring it. My memory's getting sorely challenged." He grumbled, "Oh damn, I thought sure I'd—ah." He pulled from his inside coat pocket a small jewelry box. "I usually wear it around my neck, which would make it a trifle awkward to show you when we're trussed up in these snooty environs." He opened the box. Something was wrapped in paper-thin, purple silk which his long, arthritic fingers carefully folded back.

"What is it, sir?"

Zachery's voice had humor but also reverence. "Never been precisely certain, Matthew. Supposedly it protects the bearer. It's one of my favorite relics." He lifted up a very delicate gold chain, hanging from it was a disk about the size of a fifty-cent piece, but bronze and clearly ancient. He held it carefully.

"Seems big for an ancient coin." Matt was intrigued. "A medallion maybe?"

"Perhaps."

Matt tried to focus through his champagne haze; he leaned closer, seeing a profile of a head with a face on both sides. "Looks like the Roman god, what was his name? Janus?"

"I've thought that, too," the older man said while eyeing it closely through his wireframes, "but it was found in ancient Sumer." He turned the relic over, showing that the reverse side had the same Janus-like image. Matt saw both sides of it had a tiny barb in the middle. "Considered to be some kind of ancient good luck charm. I started carrying it as a joke on myself, but it evolved into a habit, for decades."

"It's clearly been effective, sir," Matt pointed out. "You've done spectacularly."

Zachery waved off that idea. "Which may all have happened by merely being in the right place at the right time. Let me show you something else about it." He reached his left hand out. "Lay your right hand on mine, palm up."

Matt did so as Zachery leaned closer and placed the talisman into Matt's palm. With scientific enthusiasm the professor said, "Now this can be interesting—if it even works this time—it doesn't always."

From the nearby crystal shaker, he sprinkled a pinch of salt onto the talisman, then touched the tip of a finger into his water glass, transferring a droplet onto the relic. Then he placed his right hand overtop Matt's, took a slow breath, and suddenly clamped it tightly —making Matt flinch—as Zachery whispered in a language Matt had never heard...

"Awat ah-lone sin yah, tahm walla tey rek-wee."

Matt was startled to feel an electrical jolt! "Whoa! It's hot! It's —" He inhaled sharply, felt as though a gust of wind blew against him. His body shuddered as the room suddenly plunged into darkness. Where Zachery's face had been was instead the face of an unknown old man, in medieval clothes, a patch covering his right eye with ugly, clawed scars above and below it. The left eye glared fearsomely at Matt. The searing image lasted only an eye-blink, followed by a nanosecond where Matt hazily saw himself at the table—as though through Zachery's eyes. Then a lightning flash blinded him.

Matt gasped and squinted tightly. Zachery released his grip and Matt slouched back in his chair, staggered, mumbling, "...Holy sh-shit!" He glanced around nervously; fearful he'd made a scene. But he was surprised that no one had noticed. Everything seemed perfectly normal. The cocktail pianist played quietly.

Zachery laughed quietly. "Well, looks like it *did* work this time." He put the talisman back into its case and his pocket. His eyes gleamed pleasantly as his deep voice continued, "Surprising little biochemical reaction, isn't it?"

"Uh…y-yeah." Matt blinked, still thunderstruck. "'Surprising' for sure." He brushed the hair off his forehead. "I saw a strange man, w-with an eye patch."

"Really?" Dr. Zachery looked quizzical as he sipped his champagne, joking, "Did he have a parrot on his shoulder?"

"No… What caused that kind of—?" He noticed a drop of blood on his palm.

Zachery also saw it. "Oh no, did you get nicked? I'm so sorry. Couple of sharp points on that relic." He dabbed Matt's hand with a napkin.

"Looks like you did, too, John."

Zachery saw that his own palm also had a spot of blood. "I'll be damned. Too much champagne and enthusiasm. Please accept my apology, Matthew."

Two waiters arrived carrying plates with artistically presented entrees they announced to be vegetarian lasagna for Matt and for the doctor, his pancreatic sweetbreads.

Matt was still recovering. "What…was that language? Those words?"

The older man smiled nonchalantly. "Little Sumerian blessing."

"Meaning…?"

Zachery had taken a bite of his organ meat, enjoying its rich, succulent flavor. "Basically, it translates as, 'May you live a thousand years, and may the last voice you hear be mine.'"

Zachery's eyes seemed to glitter as he raised another toast to the young man.

Matt managed a crooked smile, lifted his glass.

Clinked.

~~~~

OUTSIDE, THE NOVEMBER AIR HAD A WINTRY SHARPNESS. FOG had crept in from the harbor. Still slightly woozy from the champagne and his strange experience, Matt stepped to the curb. He waved at the nearby limousine which had picked him up earlier before collecting Dr. Zachery where he landed at the East River helipad. Matt glanced back at the Tower Court skyscraper looming up into the lowering night sky above Zachery, who stood on the building's front steps. His long, black evening coat wafted in the wind like dark wings of a flying predator, Matt thought, as Zachery moved down to the street. Matt opened the limo's rear door.

"Thank you, Matthew." Zachery shook his hand, swallowing a small cough as he bent into the cab, complaining, "Ahk. Very creaky tonight." He settled in, referencing the uniformed driver. "Are you certain you don't want him to take you home, Matthew?"

"Yes, sir, I'm sure." Matt was still trying to find his sea legs. "I really n-need to walk. Thanks again, Doct—" he caught himself. "*John*. For everything."

Zachery smiled warmly. "It's my pleasure, Matthew."

Matt smiled back, closed the door, and the limousine glided smoothly away. Matt stood alone on the blustery street. He shivered, glanced up toward the restaurant, but the increasing fog now enshrouded the top. Matt fancied that the building seemed to be leaning slightly toward him. He muttered, "What the hell happened up there?"

He shook his head and started walking a block east. He was braced by the frigid air, but still buzzed by the champagne plus his good fortune. He smiled, until he turned the corner to head north on Trinity Place, where he slowed to a stop. The street ahead was very foggy. But something else was far more curious. A block ahead of him, moving toward Old Trinity Church, was a funeral procession consisting of a horse-drawn hearse and several carriages. Their horses had black ostrich plumes. All the mourners, including those on foot, were dressed in late-Victorian clothing.

Whoa. Somebody making a movie about 1899? Matt blinked. Wondered why he was inexplicably certain of that specific year. Then he realized that the procession seemed to be moving in dreamlike slow motion. Several Victorian mourners glanced directly back at Matt or perhaps someone behind him.

He glanced back over his shoulder but saw nothing unusual. When he looked north again on Trinity, the foggy street was empty except for a few cars and a handful of present-day pedestrians.

Matt stood still, confused. Contemplating the phenomenon. Then he walked slowly on. Reaching Trinity Church and its graveyard with wisps of fog fingering through tombstones, he eyed it curiously as he passed.

Continuing north, he passed the 9/11 Memorial. Turning west on Chambers and crossing West Broadway, he was puzzling over the funeral he'd just seen—or imagined. He paused to glance back over his shoulder. The fog had lifted enough that the skyline of Lower Manhattan was slightly clearer, twinkling. One World Trade Center gleamed.

As he cut north across tiny, triangular Bogardus Park toward Hudson Street, Matt had an eerie sense that something felt wrong. He slowed to a stop, frowning, trying to understand what he was sensing. He closed his eyes tightly then looked back downtown again and what he saw drained the blood from his face.

All of the newer buildings, including the Trade Center, had disappeared. The much-darkened skyline looked like it might have in the late 1930s. Looming in the night sky overhead was a huge Graf Zeppelin with a Nazi swastika on it. He recognized from old newsreels: it was the *Hindenburg.*

Matt was aghast, muttering, "What the hell?!" He stumbled backwards, fell onto the sidewalk. When he dared to look back up, there was no eight-hundred-foot dirigible. The contemporary skyline of the Battery was solidly in place. He looked around at the few people also walking nearby, behaving with complete normalcy.

Matt rubbed his eyes, nervously brushed the hair off his fore-head. Got to his feet. Glanced again at the skyscrapers, then walked more quickly up Hudson, keeping his focus ahead. For eleven minutes there were no more incidents. He was beginning to think he might be okay if he just never drank champagne again.

He was almost to Houston when he suddenly had a vaporous double-vision, like the pentimento effect where beneath the surface of a painting, the image of an earlier painting on the canvas could be faintly seen, hidden behind the new work. Gazing up the real-world Hudson Street, Matt was also seeing a pale, quavering, ghostly vision of what seemed like a broad, flat helipad facing shadowy Governors Island across the foggy, dark waters of New York Harbor. He felt as though he was walking across the tarmac toward a blurry helicopter with its engine revving up, blades begin-ning to rotate until a chill gust of wind dissipated the vaporous images and Hudson Street became normal again.

Matt was confounded by why these phantasm visions were creeping into his mind. Continuing to walk, Matt suddenly felt more unsteady, as though trying to maintain his balance while gravity shifted beneath him. He heard the faint sound of a heli-copter approaching from behind him then had another fleeting pentimento-like glimpse as though he himself was five hundred feet airborne and banking so steeply northeast over the Hudson that it was vertigo-inducing.

Suddenly dizzy, he sat on a bus bench, closed his eyes. But the bench felt like *it* was moving, rocking. He put his hands down onto each side to steady himself. Opening his eyes, he experienced the strangest vision yet.

He was sitting inside the front of a small, rustic wooden wagon with a round roof. It was rocking along on an uneven dirt road, being pulled by a single horse, ridden by a cloaked man. The surrounding plain was barely visible in ethereal moonlight. As the wagon turned slightly, two men in medieval clothes came into view.

Matt saw they were standing up from a small campfire in the middle of a circle of gigantic stones.

It was Stonehenge. Matt was somehow aware the year was 503 *anno Domini.*

His vision swirled as the wagon stopped, the coachman dismounted and reached to assist his passenger—whose eyes Matt was looking through. That passenger's frail, elderly hands came up into view, grasping the coachman's hand. The image slurred closer to the fire where the two men looked into Matt's eyes, nodding respectfully. One seemed to be a peasant farmer whose weather-beaten face showed years of hard work. He wore a thick sheepskin coat over his drab gray tunic and brown woolen hose. Matt saw the other was a well-fed indoorsman, perhaps a tavernkeeper, wearing a thinner goatskin coat over his red tunic, belted with a sash. His skin was smooth. The two lifted up and supported between them a younger man, about nineteen, clothed like the farmer, who'd been lying on the earth. He was barely conscious.

Matt's point of view moved closer, only inches from the youth's face, examining him minutely. Matt's gnarled fingers stretched, squeezed, and prodded the boy. The old hands tore open the youth's shirt to examine his muscular chest.

There was a blurry transaction of small gold coins in a pouch from the coachman to the tavernkeeper. Then the coachman lifted the youth's right hand, placed it palm up atop Matt's aged left hand. Matt saw his aged right-hand fingers place the Janus talisman into the boy's palm then tightly clasp the relic and the boy's hand.

Matt stared straight at the young man, heard a high-pitched, raspy voice speaking the same strange phrase Zachery had.

The youth gasped. Convulsed violently. For a brief instant Matt was *seeing through the youth's eyes.* He saw the face of the man with the patch covering his clawed-out eye. His bloodshot left eye glared at Matt with an expression of terror.

"Hey!" a woman's voice shouted.

Matt blinked. He was sitting on the bus bench. Looking at the open door of a bus that had arrived. The bus driver said impatiently, "You gettin' on or ain't ya?"

Matt shook his head. The door hissed closed, and the bus departed.

He took a moment to look around, to get his bearings. Then he stood shakily, walking another half-block on Hudson. Approaching the Houston Street corner, he grew more unsteady. He leaned against a lamppost, closing his eyes. His brain was swimming through murky confusion. He heard angry, muddled voices.

Looking across Houston Street he saw a big sign on a storefront advertising BRAND NEW FOR 1999!—THE FORD TAURUS!

It seemed the same corner—but over twenty-five years earlier? A tall man with wavy brown hair wearing a blue windbreaker jacket was shouting angrily, walking right up and getting into Matt's face. The tall man's face was obscured by shadows, his words distorted, but furious. His hands grabbed at Matt's collar and though Matt felt nothing, his vision jostled, triggering vertigo. Matt stepped off the curb—right in front of an oncoming car that blared its horn at him. Matt stumbled back onto the sidewalk. When he glanced up the tall angry man had disappeared. The 1999 ad was gone. Instead, Matt saw a present-day couple cheerfully cleaning up after their small Goldendoodle.

Matt was panting, his brain twisting. He forced himself to walk east on Houston.

By the time he reached Bleeker, he felt like he was looking through the wrong end of binoculars. Like he was walking in a bad dream. More confused than ever, he was struggling to remember his building's address, muttering, "Was it 714, or—?" He felt frightened. Getting to the corner he recognized the red brick building at the familiar address of 417. But it was the entrance to a clothing store. Befuddled, he looked around the corner at Bank Street and was relieved to recognize the single narrow door with the number 82, the side entrance to the apartments where he lived.

Up in their flat, Dev was wearing an ancient THE TRUTH IS OUT THERE tee-shirt, happily looking at a fuzzy UFO photo on his computer as Matt entered. Dev remained attentive to his screen. "Hey! Check it out, man! This guy in Kanab, Utah is live-streaming a shot of a no-shit UFO!"

He didn't see Matt close the door and lean his fevered forehead against it, saying, "Something's wrong."

"Of *course* there is," Dev agreed, focused on the UFO. "Aliens, paranormal stuff. That's what Thelma Greer was saying at Town Hall: The government wants to hush it all—"

"With me. Something's wr-wrong with *me*." He took a step and stumbled, catching on the back of a chair.

"Whoa!" Dev jumped to help. "What is up with— Hey. You've been drinking? Since when?" He guided Matt toward the tiny bedroom.

"I've been…seeing things."

"Yes, yes," Dev nodded, "that does happen when your blood-alcohol level gets higher than your IQ."

Matt was blinking heavily, mentally stressed. "Like memories… but they couldn't be. Then two men fighting. And I swear to God, I *remembered* it. Like one of them was *me*. But back in the 90s!"

"Before you were born?" Dev's eyes brightened. "Cool! I could get you on the *Sightings* podcast!"

"I'm s-serious, Dev… And I feel like in the air flying somewhere right now!"

"You are, pal: on the redeye flight to dreamland." Dev eased Matt down onto his futon.

Matt heard Dev's voice echoing oddly, "Just beam yourself down onto your elegant four-poster here and sleep it off."

Matt's heavy lids couldn't fight it any longer. He slipped into delirium. His vision spiraled into darkness along with his lapsing consciousness.

Then he heard ocean waves as jumbled dream fragments faded in and out inside his brain.

Matt saw the bow of an 1850s ship cutting through the choppy ocean. His point of view swung around to a scruffy, bosky-bearded seaman who saluted him. Matt saw the ship's deck was covered with grief-stricken African slaves, bound in chains.

Then he was sipping champagne, eying the comely stewardess aboard the Concorde. And with a swoosh Matt's mind's eye was suddenly looking out from the podium at an audience of graduate-level students in a 1990s lecture hall. They were cheerily looking at Matt, laughing appreciatively at something he'd said.

Then, in a blur, came glimpses of the 1899 funeral at Old Trinity Church, which in Matt's brain morphed kaleidoscopically into an austere 1600s Salem courtroom seen through Matt's eyes as though he were the judge. A desperate woman held tightly by impassive Puritan guards was crying hysterically, wringing her hands to him for mercy until a momentary flash of the one-eyed man at Stonehenge interrupted and the image blurred into a nineteen-year-old 1400s French girl glaring directly at him from where she was being burned at the stake. Her widening eyes were focused on him intensely, unwavering, even as the searing flames ignited her hair.

Then Matt's internal eyes blinked and he saw a whiskey-smuggling warehouse filled with 1930s trucks and underworld goons wearing suits and fedoras. They nodded respectfully, directly into his eyes. His point of view swung to see a brassy redheaded woman gazing provocatively at him from the shiny black fender of his 1935 Packard. Flashes came of sex with her, then many different women, including rustic medieval peasants, a shimmery 1920s flapper, a Shakespearean courtesan. Several women fearfully fought against his groping: an African slave and a shadowy, frightened blond, the walls around her seeming to pulsate with firelight.

Then he was on 1999 Houston Street, struggling with the tall man, before a lightning flash of the horrific one-eyed man was followed by unfathomable darkness.

Chapter 6

As he slowly drifted back up from the depths of sleep the first curiosity Matt noticed was an unusual sour taste in his mouth. There was also a faintly odd scent in the air around him. Stale tobacco? Matt registered both while his eyes were still closed. And he felt peculiar. His body was achy, with a heavy feeling in his arms and legs. His skin seemed sensitive to touch. Slowly opening his eyes, he was surprised to see darkness surrounding him. Yet he instinctively felt it was morning. He reached out his right hand into the darkness and his fingertips touched a hanging cloth.

Lifting his head slightly and glancing around, he could just barely discern that the darkness was because cloths were hanging down on either side and at the foot of where he laid. It also seemed that six feet over his head a dark cloth formed a ceiling. He thought it was a joke, wondered, *What the hell? Dev made a tent over me?*

He rolled onto his right side, then, with some discomfort, up onto his right elbow. He drew his legs up, let his feet swing down over the side as he pushed himself up onto the edge and realized his feet weren't on the floor beside his futon. They were dangling.

That strangeness prompted him to part the bed curtains slightly. Though it was nearly as dark outside the curtains, what he saw confounded him.

He was not in his tiny bedroom on Bleeker Street. He was in a large, gloomy, completely unfamiliar chamber. His eyes refused to focus, but there were shadowy blobs that may have been large pieces of furniture or an outsized fireplace.

Opposite where he sat on the edge of the high bed, he saw what appeared to be a tall, heavily curtained window with the tiniest sliver of light in the middle where the two panels met.

He carefully stood, shakily. His brain was straining to understand. He walked barefooted across thick carpet and used both hands to separate the curtains and peek out. It was a vista he'd never seen before, and considerably out of focus. Under a cloudy, lowering sky, expanses of green lawns and many stands of evergreen trees were interspersed with November-barren skeletons of deciduous trees. A river flowed in the distance.

But the unfamiliar landscape was not what truly stunned Matt. It was his hands on the curtains. He could see them more clearly, but they were not *his* hands.

The hands were narrow, long-fingered, wrinkled, age-spotted and darker-skinned. He lifted his right hand closer to his eyes, studying the back of it, seeing small lumps of arthritis. He pushed his nightshirt sleeve up. His forearm was bony, atrophied, dark-skinned.

Matt laughed, suddenly understanding. *Of course! I'm dreaming!*

He'd had that correct recognition before while in a dream, though this dream was more tactile, tangible, real. *Well,* he thought, *at least I didn't wake up on the ceiling as a Kafka cockroach.*

He padded slowly back across the dark room toward the old English four-poster bed, planning to stick his face back into the dream-pillow and awaken properly. But his bladder sent painful signals and an open door beckoned him toward a large, white-tiled, late-nineteenth-century bathroom. The blinds on its windows were down so it was shrouded in darkness like the bed chamber. Getting closer he could distinguish that a seven-foot bathtub stood to one side on four clawed feet. On the opposite wall was a low, square ceramic sitz bath. Just inside the door was an old-fashioned toilet. Standing over it he pulled up the long, gray nightgown and held it gathered in his left hand as his right hand found his penis. Without looking down he tried to urinate, but nothing emerged. He pushed harder internally, the pain in his bladder intensifying, but only a few meager drops emerged. He looked down and was startled to see that he had only a scant bit of very gray pubic hair.

But far more shocking: his penis was not circumcised.

"Wh-what the hell?" He said aloud and was startled to hear his voice—unnaturally deep and guttural. The dream was becoming a nightmare. His fear increased. "What the f-fucking hell?!"

He staggered back from the toilet, distempered, his brain reeling, both hands went to his head—and felt that his normal hair was gone. "What? *What!*" He bumped into the door frame. Beside it was a 1920s pushbutton wall switch. He punched it. On the wall across the room a light came on overtop an ornate white pedestal sink with a beveled-glass bathroom mirror which had two additional winged mirrors on either side.

Matt stared at the triple reflections and hazily saw someone gazing back at him. Moving closer, his blood chilling with every step, Matt was staring at the reflection of his face.

But it was the face of Dr. John Zachery.

"...*What?!*" Matt's voice rumbled. Because it was Zachery's voice.

Barely breathing, Matt stepped closer to the three mirrors, each reflecting the frightening alarm on the, eighty-year-old face of John Zachery.

With trembling, wrinkled fingers Matt touched his craggy, sunken cheeks, his close-cropped, salt-and-pepper black-Anglo hair, moustache and beard, the drooping lids over his rheumy gray-green eyes.

Terror surged up in Matt. His mouth gaped open—revealing that six of his teeth were gone.

Matt gasped. Tears suddenly filled his old man's eyes. "*No, no, no!*" Then his basso voice roared, bellowing, *"Th-This can't be?!"*

Matt was wild-eyed with shock and fear. He stumbled back across the bedroom, pulled the heavy curtains wider, revealing French doors that looked out across the parklike grounds to the Hudson River, all still out of focus.

Tears spilled over and found tiny channels along the many wrinkles on his face. "H-How did I get here?!" He rambled out loud desperately, near hysteria. "Where is *here?* Oh God. This can't be h-happening!"

He turned back and looked at the richly appointed room with its vaulted ceiling like the top of a sultan's huge tent. It was a deep midnight-blue with dozens of golden five-pointed stars painted on it. They reminded Matt of the little gold stars his kindergarten teacher put on his papers. That memory triggered a tsunami of despair. He felt caught in a downward-spiraling maelstrom, being sucked under dark waters, drowning in surreality. His lungs and brain were near exploding.

He rushed madly back into the marble stall shower by the bath-room sink. He twisted the hefty white porcelain faucet, and freezing cold water poured down onto him, making him gasp. He coughed badly, turned his face up into the deluge, rubbing at his cheeks, frantically trying to scrape them off.

Desperately, he pounded his hands against the marble walls, "This can't be r-real!" he shouted, "Come on! W-wake up, Matt!" He could feel his sanity shredding, his brain's neural fibers ripping apart. His panic got ever more extreme. He screamed again desper-ately, *"Wake up!"*

He slipped and stumbled from the shower, grabbing the

pedestal sink to catch himself, but was once again facing the elegant bathroom mirror, seeing the reflection of his flannel gown soaked and clinging to his octogenarian body. And that face. The nightmare face that he was trapped within.

He grabbed a heavy cut-crystal glass from the sink and hurled it —shattering the mirror as he shrieked, *"Jesus Christ, wake up!"*

He stumbled back into the bedroom, coughing, crying, howling desperately at the top of his lungs, "Help me! *S-Somebody please! Help me!"*

He heard footsteps outside. Then the bedroom door opened a crack. The butler Jamison peered in, "Sir? Were you—*Oh, sir!"*

He saw his master, thoroughly drenched, with tears streaming down his aged face, teeth missing, arms waving crazily, hands clawing at his face like a madman.

Matt rushed to clutch the butler's jacket lapels, shouting in his face, "Please! Please wake me up! *Wake me up!"*

Jamison clamped his hands atop his master's hands, spoke with assuring certitude, "You *are* awake, sir. You are quite awake."

"No!" Matt shouted, "This can't be happening! I can't be awake!"

"But you are, sir. You must have had another nightmare, sir. Try to calm yourself, Dr. Zach—"

"No, no! I'm n-not Zachery!" Matt screeched frenetically. "My name is Shaw. I'm M-Matthew Shaw!"

The butler cocked his head, faintly familiar with the name, but worried and struggling to remain professional. "I beg your pardon?"

Mucus was draining from his old man's nose into his moustache and beard as Matt pleaded, "I'm not... I'm not who you th-think I am!"

"We'll sort it all out, sir." He gently unclenched Matt's grasp on his lapels. "But please, try to calm yourself."

"I'm t-telling you my name is Matthew Shaw. I'm—" then

something registered. "Wh-What do you mean 'another' nightmare?"

Jamison lifted a bathrobe from its valet hanger, speaking carefully. "Of late, sir, you've had similar…episodes."

Matt bristled at the man's condescension. "Similar—? But that can't be! I've never even seen—" He struggled to get on top of his own turmoil. "Look, I know, I—" Matt tried to control his wheezing, to let the butler guide his frail arms into the robe. "I realize it m-must sound insane. I just—"

"No, sir, you're merely confused."

A very concerned Puerto Rican maid in her bathrobe and slippers appeared in the door, speaking to Jamison. "What's wrong?"

"Everything!" Matt shouted without looking at her, clasping both hands to his fevered head again.

Jamison gestured for the maid to open the curtains fully, brightening the room, increasing its reality. It made Matt more afraid. His arms and legs were trembling, but he willed himself to speak less feverishly. "Look. S-Something very…" his eyes were flitting about nervously, "I don't know h-how to… Something has…" Matt shook his head. "I'm s-sorry, who are you two?"

"Maria is one of our head maids," Jamison patiently reminded him, "And I am Jamison, sir."

"You work here?"

"Your butler, sir. For twenty-two years."

Matt glanced nervously around the aristocratic bedroom; his vision still unfocused. "Where is *here?*"

"At your estate, sir. In Sleepy Hollow."

Matt guffawed angrily. "Don't make *j-jokes!* What are you talking—"

"The village of Sleepy Hollow, New York, Dr. Zachery."

"No!" Matt's deep voice roared, "I am n-not Doctor—" he choked it off. He was quaking. "How did I get here?"

Jamison answered with studied calm. "You came up from the city last night, sir. By helicopter, about midnight and—"

"No! No! I walked home!" Matt declared. "Up to Bleeker to—" Matt suddenly laughed idiotically, more tears of pure terror overflowed as he turned in a circle, taking in the whole scene, bleary-eyed. "Oh God, this isn't happening. This all *c-can't* be happening! I —" He suddenly coughed violently, flinching. Jamison caught his arm, guided him to a carved wooden chair with a thick red leather seat and eased him down.

The maid took a step closer. "Is it the pain?"

"Perhaps," Jamison replied as he attended the old man. "Is it hurting, sir?"

"What?! No!" Matt stammered, "I mean y-yes, there's some pain, but I'm just—"

"Did you forget to take your medication?"

"No! I don't have— What m-medication?!" he frowned.

"For the pain, sir."

Matt snapped harshly. "For what fucking pain?!"

Jamison took a breath, spoke softly. "…From the cancer, sir."

Matt's blood became icy. He stared at Jamison, who patiently, gently continued, "The cancer in your lungs."

~~~~

IN THE BLEEKER FLAT, DEV WAS HURRIEDLY SPOONING THE last bite of oatmeal with raisins into his mouth with one hand while putting his bowl into their tiny kitchen's overburdened sink. He shouted, "Hey! Are you awake, man?"

Matt's voice came back. "Yes, Dev."

"There's oatmeal left if you want it." Dev glanced in the mirror on their living room wall, giving a quick brush up to the hair pile on his head. Grabbing his yellow coat and backpack he opened Matt's bedroom door slightly, peering in. "You okay?"

His longtime pal was resting comfortably on his back atop the futon, still in last night's clothes. He smiled at Dev. "Never better."

"Glad to hear it." Dev headed for the front door, calling back, "And I def want to unpack all that spooky stuff you were rambling about last night. Catch you later." Then he left.

His roommate stretched luxuriously, repeating, "Never. Better."

He breathed a supremely contented sigh.

~~~~

JAMISON CONTINUED TRYING TO CALM HIS ELDERLY MASTER who was sitting restlessly in the bedroom chair. "Slow, deep breaths, sir. You remember how the doctor said your disorientation and discomfort would be getting worse when you reached this point."

Matt's voice was low, worried. "What s-stage is it?"

The compassionate butler hesitated. "...Advanced, sir."

Matt whispered insistently, "What stage? ... Four?" Jamison reluctantly nodded. Matt's jaw worked, but no sound emerged.

"Keep breathing slowly, sir," the butler said. "I'll get your medication." He collected the small bottle and the wireframe glasses from the nightstand. Then he used a tissue to pick up two U-shaped dentures from a dish. Matt put on the glasses, clearing his vision. He studied the false teeth, three for the top, four spaced out for the bottom. He had no idea how to insert them.

The maid came near, with a tiny respectful curtsy to Matt. She pulled the glass stopper out of a Waterford crystal decanter and poured water into its matching glass. The butler opened a prescription bottle like Zachery had held at dinner.

Matt saw the pills, frowned. "But…the capsules at dinner were y-yellow. Those are—"

"Blue, sir, yes," Jamison said with delicacy to his longtime master. "It's been a perplexing morning for you, sir, I know. Formerly you did take yellow meds, but please believe me, blue is the correct new prescription. You yourself gave them to us two weeks ago to dispense." He placed the bottle in Matt's hand, then stood upright. "Please take one, sir, and we'll get your breakfast."

Matt nodded blankly.

Jamison bowed politely, escorted the maid out, easing the door closed.

Matt stood and went to the door, listening. He could barely hear the maid saying, "This is much worse than his other Alzheimer days. Or last week, when he thought he was William what's-his-name?"

"Sanger. William Sanger."

Inside the bedroom, Matt stopped breathing.

"But that passed almost instantly," Jamison said. "This is far more intense. As we were warned it might become: convinced that he is someone else entirely."

Inside the door, Matt sagged, knowing, *That is the reality.*

He heard Jamison sigh. "I'm afraid he'll be going downhill rapidly now. Where's Nurse?"

"Still on her morning walk."

They moved away, voices growing fainter as Jamison said, "Send her to me as soon as you see her because we'd all better review the necessary…"

Matt opened the door a crack, but they were too far away to hear more. He closed the door, then looked down at the blue capsules in his hand. He was fearful of taking them. Fearful of everything.

~~~~

At that same time in the Bleeker Street flat, Dev's roommate was still resting contentedly on the cheap futon. When his blue eyes opened, they shined with extreme pleasure.

Despite the young face and body that presented itself externally as Matthew Shaw, the inside was entirely possessed by Dr. John Zachery.

The *nature* of the devious internal Zachery did manifest itself very subtly, however. Those youthful eyes now contained a shrewd glint, an edgy strangeness.

Zachery looked around slowly, took delight in his surroundings, then drew a breath. With his now-younger, higher-pitched vocal cords, he spoke with elation, "Yes!"

Zachery inhaled deeply, held his hands up to admire their smoothness. Clenched his fists. Then he sprang up from the futon feeling thoroughly rejuvenated. He eagerly peeled off the previous night's clothes and stood naked before a mirror. He turned this way and that, savoring the reflection of his young, firm, athletic body. His right hand cupped his testicles, greatly enjoying the feel of them, then his youthful fingers examined his healthy, circumcised penis and finally gripped its shaft tightly in his fist.

He was thirsty, so he looked into the small refrigerator, saw only orange juice. He reluctantly took a big swallow. His nose turned up sourly. He thought, *Must get some pear.*

Stepping into the bathroom he leaned over the ratty toilet. His urine streamed out instantly, healthy and strong. He exhaled with relief thinking, *Ah yes. Nothing quite as pleasurable as pissing like a racehorse.* He relished the experience. He then splashed cold water into his young face. He stared at his reflection, mulling his conquest and the future it represented, as he pulled contemplatively at his lower lip.

Still stark naked, he stepped over to pick up Dev's old landline phone. He was about to punch in a number when he had an amusing thought. Going back to the bedroom, he rifled through Matt's clothes, pulling out the wallet with NYU ID cards. He found Matt's cell phone. As he lifted it up the screen came to life with the words, *Face ID*—and instantly the phone recognized Matthew Shaw.

Zachery smirked, then sucked air through his teeth as he dialed. He listened, then punched in password letters and numbers. He heard a virtual voice respond, "Thank you. Your security code has been accepted. Please listen to all the upcoming choices because menu options have recently changed."

Zachery went through a lengthy series of choices, additional password verifications, until after entering a final code the voice said, "Thank you. All operations have been confirmed. We thank you for being a valued customer. Goodbye and have a nice day."

"How about a nice *life?*" Zachery was completely, arrogantly pleased with himself. He flopped back on the futon and laughed jubilantly.

Chapter 7

Beneath the vaulted, midnight-blue ceiling in the mansion's master bedroom the old man harboring the frightened young man inside was sitting on the red leather chair. A rolling service table nearby held his elegant breakfast tray atop its white tablecloth. The plates were still covered. The meal untouched. Matt had only drunk a glass of what tasted like pear juice to quell the sour tastes in his mouth. It hadn't helped.

He sat with a thousand-yard stare, but his sharp mind had been racing, going back over every minute detail of his conversations with Zachery. Though it was beyond bizarre and seemingly impossible, Matt understood that he had become the victim of some unknown metaphysical alchemy triggered by the inherent power of the strange relic that—

"Where is it!" He stood up quickly, instantly feeling painful aches in his aged back and knees from having sat. He scanned the opulent room without seeing what he was looking for. He saw a door beside the bathroom. Opening it revealed a walk-in cedar closet with a wealth of different clothing on hangers, shelves, and in drawers. A shoe rack displayed two dozen pairs. What he was looking for was on a valet rack near the other hanging garments: the clothes Zachery had worn last night. Matt rifled through the pockets but they were empty. Then on a nearby shelf he saw a segmented tray holding the gold Rolex, the money clip, receipts from the dinner and what he was looking for: the small jewelry box. His trembling fingers snapped it open.

It was empty.

"Shit!" He shouted. "Shit! Shit! Shit!" He hurled the box away then pounded his fists against the wall on either side of a small mirror. He glared at his reflection in the mirror—the craggy eighty-year-old face of his nemesis glared back at him. He pounded his fists again then turned away in a fury—but suddenly stopped. Something registered.

Matt looked back into the same mirror, focusing on his sinewy neck. With both hands he tore open the top of his gray flannel nightgown and was rewarded to see a thin gold chain around his neck. He pulled the chain up and brought the talisman into his hand.

Quaking with excitement, he examined it. With his nerves on edge, he sank onto a low, cushioned stool in front of the shoe rack. He stared at the relic trying to fathom how this could have happened. How it might be reversed.

Matt knew the talisman had some inconceivable metaphysical power that caused this nightmare. Matt wondered if there could possibly be a simple solution. With trembling hands and closed eyes he lifted the chain ceremoniously, carefully raising it up and off of his neck.

Then he reached out, placing it an arm's length away on a low shelf.

He waited nervously.

Nothing changed. He choked up, muttering, "Oh God... Please."

A hot, fearful tear spilled down his furrowed cheek. He stood. Never taking his eyes off the relic, he backed slowly, respectfully out of the cedar closet, whispering, "Please...make it go away."

But still, nothing changed. His anxiety suddenly intensified, his fingers dug into his cropped hair, his entire body became rigid. He was straining to breathe, at the razor's edge of a nervous breakdown.

Then a knifepoint of pain stabbed his lungs and he gasped, "Oh! ... *Oh!*"

He clutched his chest, sagged to his hands and knees—not praying, but grimacing in anguish, certain now that the body he was dwelling within was indeed diseased.

~~~~

THE SMALL BATHROOM IN THE BLEEKER FLAT HAD RUSTY plumbing and cheap fiberglass walls with cracks. It was thick with steam. There was a semi-opaque plastic *Stranger Things* shower curtain dominated by a dangerously menacing, fiery night sky with four silhouetted figures walking beneath it. In the narrow stall behind the curtain, hot water showered on Zachery, who was singing exuberantly in his full young voice from Rossini's *Barber of Seville* while he masturbated with lusty enthusiasm.

"Bravo a Figaro, Bravo Bravissimo," he pumped himself harder as he repeated in rhythm with increasing intensity, "Bravo Bravo *Bravo Bravo BRAVO!*" until he hit the peak and ejaculated, shouting, "Yes, yes, yes! *Yes!*" as the crest passed over him.

Then he leaned back against the fiberglass wall, panting and laughing with delight, enjoying the afterglow.

A few moments later, he stepped out of the bathroom with only a towel over his well-honed shoulders when Dev's phone rang quietly twice. Then the vintage digital answering machine picked up and Zachery faintly heard the outgoing message, "Hey. This is Dev. I am *still* out looking for The Truth. Leave word."

Zachery recognized his mansion's number on the caller ID as Zachery heard his former, old man's bass voice saying, "Dev. Pick up. Please. Your cell's m-mailbox is full again but if you're there I really need to—"

Zachery grinned impishly, clicked off the machine as he answered. "I'm afraid Dev's not in."

In the estate's bedroom, Matt was disconcerted by hearing *his own* voice answer, two octaves higher than the voice he now possessed. He swallowed hard, choked with emotion. "W-What have you done to me, you bastard?!"

"Made you famous overnight, son." Zachery picked up a pickleball, squeezed it. "You're an important historian now. Published author and—"

"A dead man walking! But this is impossible!"

"Obviously not," Zachery said cheerily.

"Y-You have to reverse this! You have to—"

"Certainly. I'll be right there." He chided quietly, "Get a life, Matthew."

"I want my own!"

"Sorry, that one's taken." Zachery admired his smooth, healthy fingernails.

"No! For God's sake!" Matt shouted. "You can't do this to me! Y-You're dying!"

"No, no, no. You are," Zachery reminded, then asked, genuinely curious, "How's the pain, incidentally?"

Matt grew furious. "I'm going to call the goddamned police!"

Zachery was eyeing his now-perfect teeth in a mirror. "I'm sure they'll be most understanding, 'Dr. Zachery.'"

Matt bellowed, *"Who are you?!"*

"Matthew Shaw."

"You can't get away with that! I know things about my life that—"

"Of course you do. Because *'You'* Dr. Zachery, had a private detective shadowing *'Me'* for months. Recorded clandestine video, audio. Listened in on 'my' conversations." Zachery pulled his lower lip. "I think it's actually rather perverted, 'Dr. Zachery,' but I'm very grateful for all your financial support. And I'm distressed that your mind is going. I definitely know that Jamison—"

"Y-You son of a bitch!" Matt was pacing, enervated.

"—That Jamison, Maria, Nurse Ratchit and others up there have noticed you becoming increasingly Alzheimer/dementia-ridden over the last few weeks—"

"Because you were playacting for them!" Matt boiled over; his deep voice dangerous. "I'll k-kill you, Zachery! I swear to God! I'll—"

"Just contemplate *that* image." Zachery shook his head. "You draining the life out of this fine, mint-condition body? What a waste. And where would that leave you, anyway?"

Matt was seething. "I swear I'll find a way to make you—"

"Can't be done, son," Zachery said with complete assurance. "Now I really must let you go, but I've arranged things so you'll be comfortable up there. And I do hope that the end comes for you as painlessly—and quickly—as possible. *Au revoir!*"

Zachery hung up.

"Hello! *Hello!*" Matt slammed the phone down. "Shit! *Sh-Shit!*"

He was in a cold sweat. Quaking. He brushed the nonexistent hair off his forehead. His eyes darted around. His frightened mind raced. "No. No. No." He stared at the phone. Had an inspiration. Then tried to remember, "What was it, LaGuardia and…and—?"

~~~~

ATTORNEY GARY DEAKINS WAS IN A WORKOUT TEE AND shorts. He was toweling sweat off his face while stepping away from others on exercise equipment facing windows that overlooked mid-Manhattan from a high floor. His other hand held his cell. "Of course I'll take it, Brenda." He listened as she patched him in. "Hey John, how are you?"

He heard Zachery's familiar deep voice respond, "I'm in b-big trouble, Mr. Deakins."

The lawyer's face wrinkled quizzically, "'*Mister* Deakins'?"

Standing over the phone in the estate bedroom, Matt flinched, regrouped. "Uh...G-Gary. Sorry. It's been kind of a weird morning."

Deakins was concerned. "Sorry to hear that, John. What's going on?"

"S-Something unexpected has happened." Matt tried to sound as businesslike and officious as possible. "It's very important that you stop the s-scholarship for Matthew Shaw. Stop any of Zachery's...I mean *my*...money from going to him. Immediately."

Deakins drew a sympathetic breath as he stepped into a quieter reception room also enhanced with mid-city-vista windows. He spoke softly, "It's gotten that bad, John?"

Matt was confused. "Wh-What?"

"The pain. And the effects of all your medications."

"No." Matt shook his head, paced as he held the receiver. "No, you d-don't understand, it's—"

"Just like you told me it might be, John? That the pain and drugs might give you some panicky second thoughts or—"

"No!" Matt flared, but immediately sucked it back, forcing himself to speak calmly. "No. That's not it. I have no second thoughts about the other three students, I just..." he was thinking fast, "...just came into disturbing new information about Shaw and ch-changed my mind. So I want you to stop—"

"John," Deakins sighed, sitting against the back of a chair, gazing out sadly at Manhattan's eastside skyline. He spoke gently. "You told me—repeatedly, old friend—to *ignore* you, if anything like this happened."

"Yes." Matt realized how remarkably shrewd his adversary had been. "Well, things have changed…dramatically, so now I'm telling you to—"

"You specifically said," the attorney quietly reminded him, "that I should 'treat you like Ulysses tied to the mast of his ship as the Sirens sang.'" He turned his cell speaker on and opened a search window.

"Forget all that, dammit!" Matt was getting scared, but still trying to walk the necessary tightrope. He tried to gain some strength from his deeply sonorous voice. "Here's the deal, Gary, you're my lawyer and I want you to stop any of my money from going to—"

"But you already sent your confirmation codes into the system this morning." Deakins was eyeing the info on his search.

"No! That's ridiculous," Matt fumed, "I never sent any—"

"John…John…" his soothing voice was maddening to Matt, "I'm looking at the screens right now. The educational trusts for the other three students are completed." He switched to another screen. "And all the transfers to the special new account at JPMorgan Chase—the *separate estate trust* you and I created especially for Matthew Shaw—they have also been completed. It's a done deal exactly like *you* wanted, old friend. Now try to—"

"I'll s-sue your ass!" Matt shouted. "I'll get another attorney! I'll—"

"Oh John," Deakins' voice remained calm and sincerely sad, "I am so sorry to hear you like this. You were afraid that exactly this might happen. That's why you made our firm your trustee—gave us complete power of attorney."

Matt's heart dropped. "I did what?"

"Gave us your POA. Yes. You really don't remember?"

"Of course I don't remember!" Matt was coming unglued. "How could I f-fucking remember! I'm—"

"John," he spoke closer into the cell, "please don't do this to yourself. Everything is okay. Really. Everything is under control."

Then he added softly, but clearly and succinctly, *"Exactly like you wanted it."*

Matt was harried, stammering, "But b-but—No! You don't—"

"Please don't stress, John, there's no need," the attorney said very patiently, compassionately. "You were so happy when we finished all the paperwork. You even gave me that pricy box of Havanas—which we laughed about when I reminded you that I'd quit smoking. And listen," he added reassuringly to his longtime client, "You'll be very well cared for by the side account we set up to keep you comfortable at Sleepy Hollow. You'll have first-class assisted care until..." he paused, hating to say, "...until you no longer need it."

Matt's head was spinning. Trying to find a loophole. Anything to stop this juggernaut.

"Meanwhile," Deakins continued, "except for the scholarship accounts we created for the other three students, the rest of your entire portfolio has been successfully transferred. You yourself entered all the correct password codes, ID info and then you recon-firmed everything electronically this morning. The accounts are solidly in place now at Chase."

Matt was confused. "What do you mean my 'en-entire portfolio'?"

"That includes everything else: the Sleepy Hollow mansion and all your many properties here, in Europe and Asia, your museum-level collections, your personal monetary holdings, bonds, gold and —" Matt heard the lawyer chuckle with amazement, "Not to mention your brilliant early investments in those ground-breaking tech start-ups. It's the whole shooting match, John: all your accu-mulated wealth. You bequeathed and transferred it all to Matthew Shaw. He's one very lucky young man, receiving the entire ninety-seven billion."

Chapter 8

Bright morning sunshine streamed down onto Greenwich Village, but the November air was frigid. Puffs of breath emerged from the varying pedestrians, several of whom noticed the cheerful, chestnut-haired young man bouncing around the corner from Bank onto Bleeker. Zachery wore Matt's old jeans and skimpy jacket over a faded NYU Med sweatshirt—but he knew a much better wardrobe was forthcoming. Zachery felt energized by the rush of new youth, enjoying clear vision without glasses, healthy breathing without cancerous, withering lungs. He nearly bumped into a bakery delivery man opening his van.

"Oh, beg your pardon!" Zachery paused to beam at the sunny surroundings. "Excellent morning though, isn't it!?"

The middle-aged guy pulled out a tray of cinnamon rolls, grumbling in his Brooklynese, "I'd rodder be in Miami."

"Oh, you must think more grandly, my boy. Like perhaps, Venice! I'm heading that way very shortly!" He inhaled grandly. "And I haven't felt this fine in forty years!"

The man eyed the loony youth. "Wow. And you don't look a day over twenty-five."

"Lots of clean living." Zachery winked, grinned brightly and bounded on down Bleeker.

~~~~

MATT WAS STILL IN HIS FLANNEL GOWN AND ROBE, HIS NERVES on edge. Sitting on the low stool in the closet, he held the bronze talisman in the sweaty palm of his eighty-year-old hand. He was desperately trying to remember the strange words of the Sumerian "blessing," hoping to reverse the frightening phenomenon.

"'*Awat ah-lean*'? No. '*Awat ah-lone*'?" He drew a quick breath of encouragement. "Yes. I think that was it. '*Awat ah-lone—*' what?" His brain strained to remember the phrase. "'*Awat ah-lone…*' Shit! G-Goddamn it!"

He slammed the talisman down on the floor beside him.

~~~~

ZACHERY WAS LOOKING OUT THROUGH THE WINDOW OF Cozy's burger joint, enjoying the everyday life on busy Astor Place. The black waitress with purple hair brought two plates. "Double burger with everything. Side of chili fries. *And* pork 'n' beans."

Zachery rubbed his young hands together. "Looks marvelous, Shakila!"

She glanced curiously at her longtime customer. "Uh, Matt? … Hell-lo? … *Shakira?*"

"Of course! My dear *Shakira*." He'd misread her nametag, covered smoothly, "I was momentarily transfixed by the allure of your…pork and beans."

Shakira was savvy, picking up his sexual vibe. "Riiiight." She eyed him sideways, then gestured toward his meal. "And s'up witchu, Mattsy? Red meat?"

Zachery gobbled down a fry dripping with beefy chili. He grinned arrogantly, recited his favorite Nordic phrase, then translated for her, "Means 'What the hell,' you know?"

"You only live once, huh?"

With a cagey smile, Zachery said, "Speak for yourself." He gave her a sexy wink and lasciviously sucked the chili off a fry.

That move confirmed Shakira's suspicion. "Better watch yourself, dude," she warned him, "or I'll tell Molly you're out trollin'."

Zachery held up both hands as if being arrested. "I simply can't restrain myself, Shakira." He glanced at other customers, lowering his voice to a private whisper, "Because you've got the most delectable buns in the Village."

Her brown eyes held on his compelling blue ones. Then she raised her eyebrows, pointed her forefinger finger at him like a gun and wagged it negatively, with a forceful expression of, *Nope. We ain't going down* that *road, honey.*

Zachery understood, smirked. He watched her walk away, thinking, *We'll see about that.*

~~~~

DOWN THE HALL FROM ZACHERY'S BEDROOM, MATT HAD discovered the study. He'd seen the files with information about himself and the other three. He'd searched through myriad other folders he'd scattered on the desk, tables, and floor. Many came from an oak file cabinet he'd also opened and ravaged.

Matt's attention was now on the rolltop desk which he was tearing through relentlessly, searching for some clue about the relic or the phrase. With jaw tightly clenched he growled, "It's g-gotta be here! Written down somewhere!"

Kneeling on the floor he disgorged a few remaining pages he'd missed previously in the bottom drawer, scanning, and quickly discarding one after another until there were none.

He sagged. It was driving him mad.

~~~~

Zachery emerged from a smoke shop on Sheridan Square, a narrow triangle of greenery cordoned off by a spiked, wrought-iron fence. He saw two college girls leaning against it, talking. Zachery belched, feeling heartburn from Shakira's chili. He opened the Tums he'd discovered in Matt's jacket pocket and took one. Then he lit a cigar while watching one girl, a striking brunette, who eyed him appreciatively. He relished her interest. Puffing up, he approached, noting the book in her hand, *Leaves of Grass.*

"Ah! '*Youth, large, lusty, loving. — Youth full of grace, force, fascination.*' You ladies enjoy Walt Whitman? He was a hell of a guy, take it from me."

They smiled back, intrigued by this young collegian.

Zachery was enjoying it immensely.

~~~~

In the mansion's grand hall two floors below the study, five antiquarians were meticulously scrutinizing artifacts and noting information with subdued voices. One woman glanced up

—startled by what she saw. One by one the others followed her gaze as silence fell.

By the archway leading upstairs stood Dr. John Zachery in his bathrobe and bare feet looking like a mixed-race Ebenezer Scrooge.

Matt advanced into the chamber, thunderstruck by the bizarre collection surrounding him. He began moving quickly from table to table, touching some of the items. At the opposite entrance the maid Maria saw him picking up various papers then tossing them aside. She whispered to a housekeeper who hurried away as Maria went toward the doctor.

Matt recognized her. "Oh yes. Th-there you are...uh—"

"Maria, sir."

"Of course. I'm trying to f-find something, Maria."

"What is it, sir?"

"Just tell me, where does he keep—where do *I* keep—my m-most important papers?"

"They would be up in your study, Doctor."

"I looked there, dammit!" Matt flared, then choked it back. "I'm sorry. I'm—"

"They would definitely be up there, sir. May I help you to—"

"No." He hurried back toward the study. "It's just—s-something's wrong."

Everyone in the room watched silently.

Matt stormed back into the study, breathing labored, his chest tight. Pained. He returned to the disheveled desk, now pulling the empty drawers completely out. He squinted into the darkness of each space then rapaciously rammed his hand deeper, feeling for anything. Inside the bottom one his fingertips touched something. He felt sudden hope. "Oh!"

He withdrew a small, vintage medical vial. A symbol on its label resembled the Janus figure on the talisman. "Yes," he whispered. "Please!" There was one word: *Effugio.*

Matt recognized the Latin, searched his memory. "'Effugio… Effugium…' Escape!" He gasped with relief. "Yes! Oh thank God!"

Meanwhile Maria and Jamison were walking quickly up the staircase toward the study. She was saying, "…and he's started stuttering, sir."

"Yes. He'd warned me that might become one of his symptoms. Did you reach Nurse?"

Maria nodded. "She'll meet us up there."

In the study, Matt was still on the floor, examining the vial in his long, nervous fingers. Inside was a yellowish liquid. He started opening the vial. Then paused.

"'Escape'…from what?" He stared at the tiny bottle, suddenly fearful. "From what you did to me? … Or from living?" Barely breathing, Matt was calculating possibilities. "Is this a s-set-up, you bastard? Did you *expect* me to find this? Did you think—"

"Excuse me, sir," a female voice interrupted. "But who are you talking to?"

Matt looked up to see a nurse wearing blue scrubs had entered. Her small voice was in direct opposition to her mass. From sturdy Dutch stock, she had short, graying black hair brushed neatly back and sprayed into place like a helmet. She wore no makeup. Her neck was thick. Her hands looked like a man's. Matt thought, *That woman could go bear hunting with her fists.* He calmed himself, surreptitiously slipped the vial into his gown's pocket, then assumed a casual tone. "Uh…no one. Just mumbling. Nurse…R-Ratchit?"

She advanced slowly toward the eighty-year-old, smiling, chiding, "Now Dr. Zachery, you know we don't think that's funny."

"Uh, right. I'm s-sorry." He forced a tranquil smile as he stood up nonchalantly, spotting the small hypodermic not fully concealed in her left hand. "Very rude. I just thought I'd lost something important. Made me a l-little nuts." He sighed comfortably. "But I'm fine now."

"Good." She continued to close the gap between them. "That's very good."

Matt gestured dismissively toward the syringe. "So I have no n-need for any of that."

He tried to do his very best "serene Zachery" impression as he saw Jamison and Maria peeking in the doorway. "I do understand why you w-were all concerned. But I'm totally cool—" he vamped quickly, chuckling, "—as my students would say."

Matt took a bold chance and turned his back on the nurse, appearing to look down at his desktop. He was actually looking toward the floor behind him and saw her feet still inching toward him. He spoke with the clearest, most unconcerned voice he could muster, "Did you enjoy your walk this morning? Looks a bit n-nippy out there."

He saw her feet come to a stop and took the offensive, turning to her. "But beautiful outside. Think I might take a walk myself."

The nurse studied him, slightly mollified. "Alright. But I think you should take some more of your pain meds first." She pulled the prescription bottle from her pocket, held it out.

He took it, shook a blue pill into his hand saying, "I think you're absolutely right."

She winked pleasantly. "Let's make it two this morning."

He knew it was a command, shook out a second, poured some water from a decanter on the desk. Then he popped them in his mouth, swallowed them, opened his mouth wide cheerfully showing proof, then said, "Jamison, would you pull out some walking clothes?"

"With pleasure, sir." He stepped away.

Taking further charge, Matt spoke dismissively to the nurse. "Thanks." He turned his back again, pulling up a chair to his desk and sitting. "I'll call you if I need you. And do close the door."

He sensed her making a last careful assessment of him, then heard her back off and exit. When the door closed, Matt retrieved the two blue pills he'd dropped on the desk and set the decanter atop before he'd faked popping them into his mouth. He put them back in the bottle.

Then he sagged back in the desk chair. He took out the "Effugio" vial, unsure of what to do. He coughed, chewed his lip. Then he noticed Zachery's laptop.

He booted it while holding down five specific keys, surprised how stiff his now-older fingers were. When a DOS screen appeared, he expertly found a back door overruling passwords. Matt was simultaneously ruminating on his recent Behavioral Psych class about Kubler-Ross's stages of confronting a grievous challenge—Denial, Anger, Bargaining, Depression, Acceptance—and how he'd blazed through them all in that one morning. He determined to add another stage: *Retribution.*

He went online to JPMorgan Chase's webpage, used several key combinations without success, but his determination was unflagging. While his fingers flashed automatically across the keyboard, Matt's facile IT mind ruled out DNS Exfiltration and was sifting at lightning speed through various brute force approaches to exploiting the flaws in critical infrastructure. He also mentally cross-referenced his dense stash of Dark Web resources on attack vectors. He was focused on a zero-day exploit that would avoid the blind-alley honeypot clickbait while not leaving behind any traceable IOC forensics.

At length he managed to trigger a DOS screen to appear within the Chase site. He'd hacked in. And felt encouraged.

He grinned. "I'm not going down without a fight, you old motherfucker."

~~~~

THE MANSION'S LARGE BUTLER'S PANTRY WAS EBONY-PANELED and contained the entire collection of dinnerware, fine china, sterling silverware and serving dishes. At his desk area Jamison was on a phone, reacting with surprise. "He called you this morning, sir?"

In the mid-Manhattan law offices, attorney Gary Deakins was emerging from his personal office talking on his cell while heading toward a conference room. "Yes, Mr. Jamison. He sounded pretty distressed to me, too."

"He went quite beyond distressed a short time later, sir. Utterly frantic, really. We were— we are—concerned he might do himself some harm."

Deakins stopped just outside a conference room where others were assembling. "Alright." He heaved a sad sigh. "Then we'd better institute the steps that John asked us to take."

Jamison understood. "Very well, sir. I'll see to it."

~~~~

ALONG WAVERLY PLACE AT THE NORTHEAST CORNER OF Washington Square, Zachery was strutting his stuff with the brunette, who was captivated by this handsome med-student and his fascinating insights.

"But by then," Zachery continued, "Whitman had returned to New York. White beard down to here." He touched his waist. "But immaculately clean. Like Mark Twain's snow-white hair. And you know what? Whitman always smelled like gardenias."

The brunette shook her head, enthralled. "You make it sound like you knew him personally."

Zachery shrugged, falsely modest. "It's a gift." He took a final puff of the cigar, stubbed it on a trashcan.

"Listen, Matt," the brunette said quietly, "I'm at the Brittany, sophomore floor, room 4B."

"I will certainly take that under consideration, Sophia." His eyes were suggestive.

Her eyes twinkled back. Then she headed across Washington Square, as Zachery enjoyed watching her.

Another female voice called out, "Hey! I saw that!"

He turned to see Molly approaching from under the arch. Zachery's heart skipped a beat. She looked even lovelier than when Sanger introduced her to him at the Alumni gathering. She had books in hand, hurrying to class.

She smiled as she reached him, joking pointedly. "Keep those blue eyes to yourself, pal!"

He grasped her arm, pulled her to a stop very close, *muy macho.* "And if I don't?"

"Whoa!" Molly blurted. "What's up with you?"

Zachery winked, grabbing her ass. "Just feeling my oats, darling."

"Oh yeah?" Molly said with a commanding tone. "Well don't feel 'em so hard. '*Dar-ling.*'"

She started off quickly. He fell in step saying, "You might enjoy it."

"I'm not so sure." She glanced at him, curious. "And what is this? Getting a scholarship turns you into Attila the Hun or—wait!" She leaned closer, sniffing, as they walked. "Have you been *smoking!?*"

"Discovered!" He laughed lightly, presenting a sheepish look as they walked. "I tried a cigar. Can you believe it?"

Molly was flabbergasted, thoroughly disgusted. *"No!"*

"Zachery's a bad influence, I guess." He noted her book. *"Newspaper Days?"*

"For a friend. Autobiography of—"

"HL Mencken. Sure. An inspired journalist, covered the

Monkey Trial." Zachery grinned. "Crusty old son of a bitch. One of my favorites. But listen, I want to talk about us going on a wonderful little—"

"Gotta wait. I'm late!"

She pecked his cheek, peeling off toward an NYU doorway, chiding back, "And get some mouthwash!"

He watched her go into the building and then he smiled with anticipation.

Chapter 9

The four-poster where Matt awakened had been made up. He was sitting nervously on the edge of its brocade bedspread with the nightstand phone held to his ear. Glancing at his reflection in the fireplace mirror, he was yet again jarred by seeing he'd become a bearded old man. From the phone he heard, "Hey, it's Molly, please leave word." Her voicemail beeped.

Matt drew a breath, but hung up. He stood, paced, rubbed his aching chest. Decided to disguise his voice by whispering. He picked up the phone but got no dial tone. He clicked it twice. Then it rang. He answered, "Yes? Hello?"

The butler asked, "Did you wish something, sir?"

"Jamison? Yes, I want to make a call and the line is dead."

Jamison was at his butler's pantry desk. "No, sir. But you wished your calls to be confined to internal only, sir."

"No. I never said—"

"In the event you exhibited any 'unusual behavior,' sir."

"Well, forget about that. Just—"

"You were very explicit, sir," the butler said gently. "I can show you the document in your own handwriting." He was holding it. "You wrote 'I want to avoid any possibly embarrassing public spectacle. Or being sent to a hospital.' You wished to remain here at home, sir, and—"

"No, no, Jamison. You can forget anything wr-written before—"

"And I just confirmed it with Mr. Deakins, so—"

"Stop!" Matt was vehement. "Forget who you confirmed it with, goddammit! Just—"

"Shall I call Nurse, sir?"

Matt stopped. Stymied. He forced himself to be calm. Tried to think.

Jamison asked, "Were the walking clothes I laid out satisfactory, sir?"

Matt looked at the gentlemanly garments hanging on a valet rack nearby. "Yes, thank you. I will take that walk. As soon as I'm dressed."

"Very good, sir. Ring when you're ready and Nurse will collect you."

"What?" Matt's expression hardened. "N-no. That's unnecessary. I'll be fine alone, so—"

"I'm afraid your written instructions are very specific that you 'must always be accompanied by—'"

"Right!" Matt snapped back, about to explode, barely containing himself. But he took a breath, remained unemotional. "Of course. Thanks, Jamison. I'll rest a bit, call you later."

"An excellent idea, sir."

Matt hung up. Stared at the phone. Looked at the door. Crossed over to turn the brass knob—as he expected, he was locked in.

His teeth clenched, his whispered voice seethed. "Zachery, you bastard." Then with an angry half-laugh he acknowledged, "You brilliant, goddamn bast—Ahk!"

He coughed, bent with pain, his hands atop his bony knees,

breathing hard. He glanced at the prescription bottle on the night stand, blue pills inside. The label read FOR PAIN.

He forced himself to look away, toward the French doors. He opened them, stepped into the chill air, onto the small stone terrace to assess possibilities of escape.

It was not promising. He was three stories up. A narrow ledge, barely a foot wide, extended from the balcony along the wall to a vertical, six-inch drainpipe twenty feet away.

Not something any sane eighty-year-old would attempt.

Matt thought, *Maybe you wouldn't, you decrepit old shit.* But for a desperate, proactive twenty-four-year-old trapped inside that aged body, it was a different story.

Matt hurried back in, bypassing the country-elegant outfit with polished tassel loafers Jamison had laid out. He combed through the cedar closet, digging out rugged, all-weather khaki pants and a cargo shirt that Zachery would have worn on archaeological expeditions. He found a thick cashmere turtleneck for underneath and lace-up short boots with rubber soles. He scooped up Zachery's wallet, ID, watch and an extra pair of wireframe glasses. He also saw a key ring with four or five keys to God-knew-what, but thought, *What the hell,* and pocketed it.

He carefully wrapped the talisman, securing it in a zipper pocket of his shirt. Then, pulling on a brown knit sailor's cap and some thin leather gloves, Matt snagged Zachery's long, dark trench coat and went out onto the balcony.

Looking all around below he saw no one except a gardener driving a tool-laden golf cart around a corner and out of sight. He rolled the overcoat into a ball, dropped it to the grass below. A long drop.

Then Matt drew an uneasy breath. He eased one bony leg, then the other over the balcony's stone railing. While holding onto the railing with his left hand, he reached his left foot onto the ledge. Turning his body slowly to the left, he pressed himself against the stone façade as he gingerly brought his right foot over to find narrow purchase beside his left.

Flat against the building, with his left cheek pressing on the cold granite and his arms stretched out crucifixion-like to give him maximum contact with the wall and help maintain precarious balance, he started inching to his right. He was barely breathing, moving one baby step at a time. He felt like it would take forever.

He was not quite halfway when a bead of nervous perspiration slid from under his knit cap and down his cheek, tickling his wrinkled skin mercilessly. He was loathe to move his outstretched hand to wipe it away. He knew however slightly that might unbalance him, could prove disastrous.

Three-quarters of the way, another bead of sweat got into his right eye, stinging, and blurring his vision. But Matt persevered. He was slightly more than an arm's length from the drain pipe when catastrophe threatened: his felt himself about to cough. He held his breath, tightened his abdomen. Only by a Herculean effort of sheer will did he suppress the cough as he reached his right hand out to grasp the drainpipe.

Being six inches in diameter, it was very hard to hold onto. But he did, tightly. He started to ease down. The tips of his boots dug at the wall for minuscule toeholds. His breath came in short puffs of vapor in the cold air. More beads of sweat stood out on his forehead despite the cold.

Ten feet from the ground, he glanced down. Mistake. He slipped and fell. His hands flailed wildly, grasping only air. He slammed hard on his back. His wind knocked out.

He lay on the grass for a long moment, heart pounding, assessing his condition. Nothing seemed broken. Finally, arduously, he pushed up, slowly regained his feet, panting hard.

He grabbed the overcoat, then skirted around the house, carefully staying below all the leaded-glass windows. He saw a four-car garage among the nearby trees, a Lexus and Mercedes inside. He scooted low, following a hedge, ascertained no one was about and entered the garage. Neither car had keys. He pulled out the key ring, but they were all house-type keys. One had a tiny letter S etched on it. But no car keys.

Shit, Matt grumbled internally as he stuffed the keys back in his pocket. *Shit shit shit.*

Then he noticed the gardener's golf cart sitting in a cubby by itself and plugged in to charge its battery.

With the key in it.

~~~~

DEV SAW THAT WASHINGTON SQUARE WAS PEOPLED BY THE usual students, families, and sightseers as he cut across but then glimpsed his nonsmoker roommate sitting casually on a bench puffing a cigar.

"Hey Mattsy! Are you kidding me?"

Zachery saw Dev, with his ridiculous hair-crown, eyeing the cigar critically. "Never tried one of these either. But I feel like I won the lottery, my boy."

Dev smiled, needling, "Wish I could say I know the feeling."

Zachery was cocky. "What, you want me to apologize for my good fortune?"

"No, once was enough."

Zachery looked at him, processing that response.

"But not all of us can take the day off," Dev jabbed good-naturedly, starting to walk. "I've gotta pick up a kidney, get it over to Jersey."

Zachery fell in step with Dev and tried for some Matt-style modesty. "It's just so strange, Dev. Suddenly having substantial funds. I mean, you know I've always been so frugal and—"

"Whoa! 'Frugal, substantial,'" Dev chided. "Fifty-dollar words. 'Course, you can afford those now. Maybe even get a warmer coat."

"The top of my list," Zachery chuckled, looking at his jacket's threadbare cuff. "Sweet old Dr. Zachery suggested that too. And since he's been so generous I might just take a semester off, maybe visit Venice or Provence—"

"Get outta here! How do you think sweet old 'Dr. Generous' will feel about that?"

"Actually, it's his idea." Zachery said with a saucy smile.

"What about Molly, man? Think she'll just wait around?"

Zachery presented an innocent expression, saying, "Gosh bro, I sure hope so." He sucked some air in through his teeth, considering the intriguing possibilities of Molly. His eyes glittered. "Or maybe she'll come along. She is exceptional."

Dev glanced at him, curious about Matt's haughty attitude. They approached a subway entrance and Dev said, "This is me."

Zachery offered a cigar. "Try one?"

"No, no." Dev waved it off. "I'll catch you later." He hurried down the steps as he pondered, *'Gosh, Bro?'*

Zachery watched Dev disappear into the underground, fully satisfied with the encounter. His hand leaned on the top handrail and again he noticed the worn cuff on Matt's thin jacket.

~~~~

AT THE SHADY CORNER OF LAWRENCE AND BROADWAY IN Sleepy Hollow, Matt had tucked the gardener's cart in between dumpsters behind a small-town pharmacy. Inside the quaint drug store, the middle-aged Asian-American pharmacist had smiled, seeing the elderly face of her longtime client. Then she carefully examined the small "Effugio" vial. "Bottle looks very old, Dr. Zachery."

"Yeah," Matt said. "I found it inside an antique. Any idea what it is?"

She eased open the stopper, very carefully took a small sniff. Her head jerked back, shocked by the smell. "Oh, my goodness! Bitter almonds. Yes!" She closed the bottle quickly, looking sharply at the old man. "It is potassium cyanide."

Matt nodded. Suspicion confirmed. "Poison."

"Very deadly. You should leave this with me."

"Okay. But I'll need to show it to some people, so—"

"I'll lock it in my vault."

"What about these?" He produced the prescription bottle of pain medication.

She read the label. "Oh, this was filled here, so—" She opened the bottle, peered in, frowned. She rechecked the label, then shook some of the blue pills into a sorting tray with concern. "This is not right."

"Not right how?"

"They should be yellow. These are not what the label says. This is Zelan."

"What's Zelan?"

The druggist was upset, typing on her keyboard. "A new medication, Dr. Zachery. Waiting FDA approval. We don't stock it yet. I don't understand how it got into that bottle."

Matt knew exactly how: Zachery had acquired it somewhere less ethical and switched medications two weeks ago. Then *faked* taking the blue pills himself while secretly continuing his correct pills.

"What's Zelan for?" Matt asked.

"It *raises* very low blood pressure."

"So if I had taken it?"

She shook her head as she typed, "A person in your precarious health? It…would have been a bad jolt to your system."

"How bad?"

Matt saw the pharmacist hedging, saying, "Possibly very bad."

"Please." Matt's fingertips touched her arm. "Lethal?"

The nervous druggist wouldn't let herself speak, but finally nodded: *Yes.*

~~~~

JAMISON MOVED WITH URGENCY THROUGH THE MANSION'S main hallway toward the marble entry foyer while on his cell. "No, Mr. Deakins. I'm not sure how long he's been gone or if— Just a moment, sir."

Maria came in the main entrance doors, the nurse following. Maria shook her head negatively.

Frustrated, embarrassed, Jamison spoke into his phone, "No sign of him outside either, sir. But we'll keep on—"

"Alright," the lawyer interrupted. He stood over the speaker-phone on his office desk. Two assistants hovered, awaiting instructions.

"You call the local police, Mr. Jamison. I'll contact a friend of mine at the state. Let's just find John and get him back to safety as quietly—and quickly—as possible."

~~~~

MATT HAD HIDDEN THE GARDENER'S CART AMONG GREENERY off the shoulder of Riverside Drive just beyond the parking lot of

Sleepy Hollow's picturesque, 1910 Tudor-Revival railway station. He dialed a number at the only remaining phone box tucked under one of the three Romanesque stone arches that supported the charming station's second story.

In the pathology section of NYU's oh-so-white Med-X lab where Matt and Dev normally worked a bleeping phone was answered by a Haitian lab tech. She stuck the phone on her shoulder while she kept entering computer data. "Laguerre. Lab One." She heard an older man's deep voice ask for Dev Bhandari. "Not here. He's on an organ run."

At the train station Matt was frustrated. "Wh-when'll he be back?"

"Dunno. It was to South Jersey. You want his cell?"

"His mailbox is full." Matt blew an angry puff. "Shit... I-I'll call back." He hung up. There were only a handful of people waiting, but Matt kept within the shadowy alcove, wanting to avoid recognition. At the ticket machine, he started to use Zachery's Amex card then realized they might be watching for it. He fed in cash, noting there wasn't much left. Collecting the ticket, Matt looked around apprehensively, particularly toward the street, watching for any pursuers. He saw the next southbound train was due in seven minutes and hoped it was on time.

~~~~

ZACHERY WALKED BREEZILY ALONG EAST FIFTY-EIGHTH Street as though he owned it, entering 600 Madison, the ultra-chic men's clothing store Canali.

Both impeccably tailored salesmen in the posh place eyed the poorly dressed student skeptically.

With a superior demeanor as though he owned the place,

Zachery tried on several sport coats, selected two, plus several shirts and pants. He pulled on a gorgeous angora sweater. Soon after, he handed three pairs of thousand-dollar shoes to one sleek salesman who scrutinized the young man's cheap clothes critically. Finally, Zachery put a black North Face Thermoball by the register, saying, "I think this should suffice for the present."

"Excellent choices, all."

"Of course they are." Zachery said, arrogantly producing Matt's new Chase card.

The salesman scanned in the final code, totaling everything. There was a pause as the salesman watched his computer, tapped another key. Waited. Then with a smug smile he held out Matt's bank card. "I'm afraid there seems to be a problem with your debit card, young man."

"What?"

"It's been rejected."

Zachery was supremely confident. "That's utterly impossible. Run it again."

"I believe twice is sufficient."

Zachery laughed it off. "There's a goddamn zillion dollars in that account as of this morning. Get your supervisor."

The salesman responded with faux-apology. "She's occupied just now. Perhaps you'd like to phone your bank?"

In the main JPMorgan Chase office at 270 Park Avenue, a frazzled assistant manager was speaking loudly into his phone because of a cacophony of other phones ringing and boisterous customers in the bank.

"Yes, Mr. Shaw, I'm afraid there is a problem. We can't confirm the money is in your account at this time."

Standing away from payment desk in Canali where another customer was being serviced, Zachery was bristling, "That's not acceptable. I know it's there! So you just—"

"I'm sure you're right, sir," the manager said calmly, "But we're currently having a systemic problem. We should be back to normal fairly soon, but—"

"What do you mean, 'systemic problem'?" Zachery demanded.

"We've experienced a moderate cyberattack. Our computer system is temporarily offline. But our cyberteam is working it. If you could check back later in the—"

"No. I need the problem remedied right this minute!"

"I'm afraid that's impossible, sir. If you'll excuse me, I have many other customers with the identical problem so—"

"Just wait a goddamn minute. What's your name? I'll have your—"

"Forgive me, but I really must hang up. Goodbye."

"Wait!" But the line was dead. Zachery was furious. He stormed past the self-satisfied Canali salesman, spewing angrily, "They had a cyberattack. I'll get this resolved and be right back. You just hold all those for me."

With quiet enjoyment, the salesman obsequiously said, "Oh, I certainly will. *Sir.*"

As Zachery steamed out the door, he heard the salesman mutter, "Little putz."

~~~~

THE SOUTHBOUND TRAIN FROM SLEEPY HOLLOW SPED ALONG the elevated rails above Harlem in the home stretch to Grand Central. A uniformed conductor walked toward the end of a coach with his concerned eyes on the elderly, half-white gentleman who was leaning one hand on the wall while his other shaky hand held a paper cup of water from the onboard tap. The conductor saw the passenger was coughing, breathing with difficulty, but could never have imagined everything the man had been through in recent hours, all of which was weighing on him.

The conductor put a comforting hand on the old fellow's shoulder, "Sir? Are you alright?"

While coughing, Matt nodded, managed to say, "Yes, sir…I'm cool… T-totally. Thanks." He swallowed hard. "Just…not as young…as I used to be."

The conductor gave him an additional pat on the shoulder, then moved on as the train passed East Ninety-Sixth Street, sliding out of daylight toward its destination in the dark underground.

For Matt, the sudden darkness outside added an extra weight to the extreme load he was struggling to bear.

Chapter 10

Annoyed to still be wearing Matt's cheap, inadequate clothing, Zachery entered the midtown JPMorgan Chase branch as irate as he'd been at Canali. He was surprised to find dozens of equally angry customers. He bullied his way to a fortyish assistant manager trying to placate clients, saying, "No, there will be no loss of principal or interest."

"Just what the hell is going on?" Zachery demanded.

She ignored the brash young man, addressing the others. "Everything will be back to normal soon. In the meantime—"

"Hey!" Zachery was outraged at being ignored. "Did you hear me? I said—"

An elegant woman elbowed in, accosting the banker. "Don't you have firewalls against computer viruses, for God's sake?"

"Yes of course we do, madam," the manager responded calmly, "but this was apparently a very sophisticated cyberattack that—"

"Sophisticated?!" an angry businessman chortled, "I heard it looked like some goddamned video game!"

"*Mortal Kombat,*" a younger man confirmed, "or *God of War!*"

"All we know is—please listen," the manager addressed all of them at once, "It was planted in our system this morning by an internet breach upstate and—"

"Your mainframe *crashed,*" the woman stated. "Admit it!"

"What?!" Zachery was furious.

A woman in a wheelchair pressed, "How long do you expect it to—"

"Not long. We're just asking for a little patience from all our valued customers—"

"How long?!" Zachery bellowed.

"We should be back online within thirty-six hours. But probably sooner."

Heated shouts and groans came from everyone. Zachery got in the woman's face. "I want to see the manager."

"Well, he's very busy as I'm sure you can understand and—"

Zachery erupted, forgetting himself, "Oh, he'll see *me* alright! I've been banking here for forty-seven goddamn years!"

The banker smiled sweetly at the obnoxious young man in threadbare clothes. "Started very *young*, did you?"

Zachery saw red. "Watch your mouth, you imbecilic twat! Now you just—"

But several armed security guards waded into the shouting crowd to quell the unruly disturbance.

Zachery pulled gruffly away from the angry mob, incensed over this unexpected glitch which left him temporarily destitute and with an annoyingly troubled stomach. Then he heard the elegant woman inform a latecomer, "They said 'a virus from an internet breach upstate' but who knows?"

Zachery glanced at her.

~~~~

IN THE SLEEPY HOLLOW BUTLER'S PANTRY, THE MAID MARIA was on the phone. "It's very nice of you to call, Mr. Shaw. I'll tell Dr. Zachery when he returns."

Zachery was on Matt's cell outside the bank. "The doctor's not up there with you?"

"Not…at present, sir." She was hesitant to say more. "But I'll keep your number and advise him."

"You do that!" Zachery clicked off. Frowned. Considered ramifications. Then another possibility occurred to him. He searched another number and called.

In a classroom Molly saw Matt's caller ID on her cell. She answered, whispering, "Hi honey. Class is starting, so talk quick."

~~~~

SHAKIRA, THE WAITRESS FROM COZY'S WITH PURPLE HAIR, WAS starting down the steps to the Fourth Street subway as an elderly mixed-race man in a trench coat and knit cap was coming up. He smiled, touching her arm as he said, "Hey, girl. What's up?"

She snatched her arm away from the weird old stranger. "Piss off, geeze-bo."

Shakira walked on down. Matt stared after her, chilled by his mistake. He turned and continued on up, feeling like a gray ghost moving through a familiar young world he could no longer really touch.

Minutes later Matt was walking as quickly as he could down Sullivan, breathing hard. He saw the NYU History Building just ahead. He stopped a short distance from the entrance, checking his watch. He knew Molly should be finishing a class. He was soon rewarded, seeing her emerge while engaged in conversation with two other students.

"No, you're wrong," she was saying. "The Scopes Monkey Trial is a *perfect* example of history colliding with journalism."

Matt was aching as he watched her approach, focused on her

friends. "And all the principal players were so clearly defined by Mencken's reporting: Bible-thumping fundamentalist William Jennings Bryan versus logical, iconoclast Clarence Darrow defending the theory of evolution. You knew exactly who everyone was and—" She trailed off as she saw her much-admired academic superstar approaching.

Matt noticed an odd expression cross Molly's face as she peeled away from her classmates. "Dr. Zachery!" She took his wrinkled hand with a warm smile. "What a surprise. How are you?"

"Could I talk to you a m-minute? It's very important."

"Well, sure! I'd be honored." She remembered something. "Oh, but I've gotta cancel a study session and my cell battery died recording my class. I'll be right out."

Matt waited nervously as she went back in the building and quickly returned, smiling. "Sorry, sir. And I couldn't get through. I'll try again up the street. But tell me what's going on."

They walked north on Sullivan as Matt began explaining the situation.

Molly listened to his story with increasing concern as they walked amid busy New Yorkers, collegians, and traffic. Finally, she stopped dead, stunned, while normal Manhattan life bustled around them. She stared into the old man's bloodshot, gray-green eyes. Her hand went to her forehead in disbelief. "That...that is crazy. It's—"

"I know," Matt agreed. "It's insane, un-unbelievable. I hear this deep v-voice that isn't mine." He pointed over her shoulder and she saw their reflections in a store window: Molly standing there beside a bearded eighty-year-old man. "I-I look in a mirror and it's terrifying." When she turned to face him there were tears welling in his eyes. "But I know wh-who I am, Moll. Who you are. And about us...about the little heart-shaped birthmark o-on your right hip, and about—"

"Oh my God…" she murmured, going pale, staring at him, struggling to see Matt inside. "Oh my God."

They continued walking slowly along the cold sidewalk with the everyday commotion and noise of real-world New York surrounding them as Matt continued the macabre, surreal tale.

As they turned the corner onto Washington Square South, beside NYU's modernist Bobst Library, Matt was saying, "Of course, I tried the lawyer. He just th-thinks I'm nuts because of the pain."

She was genuinely concerned. "Is it bad?"

"A little better since I got the right pills from the druggist. But…" As he brushed at the non-hair on his forehead, Molly took a deeply inquiring look at him. He saw the expression on her face. "I-I know. It's such an impossible s-story…I wouldn't blame you if—"

She squeezed his arm. "We'll figure it out. We will. There's got to be something we can do." Then she put her arms around him, hugged him tightly. She saw they were in front of the library and grasped his shoulders. "Wait right here. Let me call to cancel that session. I'll just be a sec."

He nodded and she hurried through the revolving door into the building. Matt looked around, aching psychologically and physically. He realized he was facing the Washington Square arch, standing exactly where he had the night he learned of his good fortune.

After several minutes, Matt peered into the library lobby. Unable to see Molly, he went inside.

Matt remembered the first time he'd entered the large interior lobby of the Bobst. It was an unexpected, eye-popping, square atrium extending up twelve stories to a glass ceiling skylight. The four walls were covered with what looked like a gold-threaded theatrical scrim through which the stacks on each floor containing millions of books could be seen. Having been there often since,

Matt knew the scrims were actually polycarbonate barriers to prevent suicides. Prior to their installation, there had been three.

Matt avoided looking directly at the spacious floor which was made up of black, white, and gray marble squares in a pattern that created a three-dimensional optical illusion. It was always vertigo-inducing for Matt, and his current mental state was shaky enough. He scanned across the room and the twelve crescent-shaped black benches arranged in pairs facing each other. He didn't see Molly among the fifty or so people present, nor at any of the help counters which lined the bottom of three walls.

He moved among students, then thought he heard Molly's voice from a side hallway. He followed the sound which resolved into words as he drew nearer.

"It was so *weird!*" Molly was saying with nervous agitation. "He told me *exactly* the kind of far-fetched story you warned me he might!"

As Matt slowly approached, Molly and the person she addressed came into view, angled away from him. Matt stopped dead, as though frozen by a blast of arctic air.

She was talking to Matthew Shaw.

"And my God, Matt," Molly said, "It was so *sad!*"

Zachery shook his head forlornly. "I know. It's sorrowful."

"And so much really personal, intimate stuff."

"That's despicable," Zachery agreed. "He must've had his investigator bug my place and heard us or even—"

"Yes, *or even saw us!?*" She was angry—and partly at him. "Just how much *did* you tell him while you were *drunk?*"

Zachery appeared remorseful, "More than I should have, obviously." He put his hand lovingly on the back of her neck. "I'm terribly sorry, Molly. I had no idea the old guy was going to become so demented or—"

"*I'm not demented!*" Matt's stentorian bass voice roared. He had blown. He stormed hotly toward them, startling Molly and nearby students. "You goddamned s-son of a bitch!"

Zachery raised his hands innocently, staying calm. His young face smiled sympathetically. "I know you're confused, sir, but—"

"I'm not fucking confused, you bastard!" Matt grabbed Zachery's jacket front. "I know exactly what happened! So do you! You d-did this to me!"

The onlookers backed away slightly, unsure how to react, as Molly jumped in. "Dr. Zachery. Don't do this."

"You stole my body, you old prick! My l-life! Tell her the truth!" He shook Zachery. *"Tell her!"*

Zachery suddenly used his twenty-four-year-old strength, spinning the old man up against a wall, speaking with great empathy. "Dr. Zachery, please. I'd never want to injure you, sir. I'm extremely grateful to you and I always will be. But it's time for you to step away now, sir, to let me move on with my life."

Matt struggled with the younger man's powerful grip, yelling desperately, "But it's *my* life!" He looked at Molly and the others. "Listen. I know it sounds insane, but he did s-some kind of ancient ritual!" Matt was frantic, determined. "Traded his old, dying body for mine! He's not Matt Shaw, *I am!*"

Two nearby students snickered. A girl whispered, "Yeah. And I'm Taylor Swift."

"Don't do that!" Zachery snapped angrily at the girl. "This gentleman may be disoriented and unstable right now, but he's a great man." Matt was infuriated by Zachery's smooth duplicity. "He's given the world important books that—"

"Wait!" Matt had recognized the girl. "Your name is Lexie! You're from New Rochelle!" She blinked as the weird old man looked at another student. "And you're Carl—no, *Kevin!* You live on Mulberry at Houston!"

Molly and the other students were stupefied. Kevin asked fearfully, "How the hell do you—"

"Because *I'm Matt Shaw!*" his bass voice boomed. He spotted a student who'd been attracted to the hubbub. "And you're Sam! You're in my biochem class with Banakowski!"

"Oh my God!" Zachery laughed loudly, with amazement. "Is *that* why you were grilling me, asking about everybody I know?"

"I didn't grill you about anything, you lying *shit! Tell them how you—!*"

Matt was suddenly struck by a powerful spasm of pain. His frail body shuddered.

"Dr. Zachery!" Molly reached over to calm him.

"Please, sir," Zachery spoke compassionately, "Don't do this to yourself."

Matt roared, making a phenomenal effort to overcome his pain as he spun and drove the young imposter to the floor, kneeled atop him in unbridled fury, grabbed his throat.

"Tell them the truth, goddammit! *Tell them what you did!*"

Molly and several of the students grappled with the aged man as a beefy security guard intervened. "You are outta here, pal!" He pulled the old man roughly to his feet, escorting him toward the door. Everyone on the atrium floor had come to a standstill, watching.

"Please don't hurt him!" Molly hurried along beside the guard. "He doesn't mean—"

"I ain't gonna hurt him," the guard growled.

"Molly!" Matt shouted back to her, "You've got to listen to me! He's n-not me. He's really Z-Zachery!"

People on the sidewalk were startled as the old man was shoved roughly outside by the guard, with a quiet, stern warning, "You come back, I call the cops."

Matt leaned against a lamppost, panting hard. Passersby gave him a wide berth.

Inside the lobby Zachery snagged Molly and was detouring her toward a side door. "You go on, I'll deal with this."

She was greatly stressed. "The poor man! It's so awful."

"It is indeed. A terrible way to spend his last days." Zachery said mournfully. "Go. I'll see you tonight."

Outside the entrance, Matt dared to peer in. He saw Molly departing toward the east side. He headed along the sidewalk in that direction.

Zachery crossed the faux-three-dimensional floor toward the front, while tagging the two students Matt had named. "Hey Kevin, Sam. Find a policeman. His name's John Zachery. Dangerous. Give them his description. I'll try to follow him."

Outside, Matt saw Molly boarding an uptown bus at the West Fourth corner and called out, but she didn't hear. He ran as best he could toward the bus as it pulled away. He followed while also trying to snag a cab. "Taxi!—*Taxi!*—S-Shit!"

Matt kept rushing up University Place, despite how hard it was, how winded he'd already gotten. Glancing back for a cab, he saw his own athletic body a few yards behind him, trotting along easily and smiling. Zachery feigned concern. "Must be getting rather fatigued, old fellow."

A block north of the square, Matt could finally run no further. He stopped, bent over, hands on his bony knees. He was gasping for breath and coughing in pain at the mouth of a narrow alley containing some dumpsters.

Zachery walked slowly around him. "I know being eighty gets tedious. And the pain must be worsening. Don't you have the pills?"

Matt took out the prescription bottle, shook one into his hand—careful not to let Zachery see it was yellow—and swallowed it. Zachery gloated; confident it was straining the older body's failing systems. "There you go," he said encouragingly. "They'll help."

"Why?" Matt was still bent over, breathless. "Why have you d-done this? Why me?"

Zachery shrugged. "You were a perfect choice in the right place at the right time, son. And as a bonus you have a particularly comely lover."

Matt's face hardened, his drooping eyelids narrowed, staring at his own young face surreally infested with such monstrous evil. His deep voice growled, "I swear to God, I'll kill you e-even if it kills me, too."

Zachery was amused, cocky. "Many have attempted, but as you see," he gestured toward himself, "I persist." Then he leaned closer offering an insider's advice. "Now, you really should terminate your shenanigans, you little fool, because you are light-years out of your league. You have no idea who you're dealing with." He easily slammed the old man hard against the grimy alley wall. "You may have escaped my mansion, but there's no escaping me. And I appreciate you saving me a trip to reclaim the relic. So just give it to me and—"

"I don't have it!" Matt shouted, struggling. "I left it back at—"

Zachery clenched him tighter, spoke with certainty. "No one in your position lets it out of reach." He was deadly calm. "*Give. It. To. Me.* Or in thirty seconds you'll be dead behind a dumpster and I'll have it anyway so—"

"Hey!"

Their heads turned and they saw a middle-aged beat cop approaching. "Is that old guy named Zachery?"

They each saw an opportunity and both shouted, "Yes!"

Zachery was surprised when Matt added, "I'm Dr. Zachery! Help me officer!"

The cop walked up. "Just got thrown outta Bobst?"

"That's right, officer," Zachery played Good Samaritan. "He's considerably confused. I followed, trying to calm him."

"No!" Matt chortled, furious. "He was threatening me! Trying to rob me."

"Trying to *help* him," Zachery said calmly.

The cop keyed his radio, "This is 717. Got that Zachery guy. Need transport."

"I'm Matt Shaw," Zachery continued, showing his student picture ID. "NYU med student. Actually, this man stole something from *me* and—"

"Ridiculous!" Matt huffed indignantly, opening his ID that matched his old face. "Look! I'm a well-known, respected scholar! He was harassing me and—"

"*Was* respected," Zachery interjected, "now sadly delusional."

"717," the radio voice crackled, "meet your wheels at Ninth and Fifth."

The cop responded, "717, copy."

"Officer," Matt stated forthrightly, "I'm professor emeritus at NYU, Harvard and—"

Zachery spoke over him, "If you just search his pockets, I'm sure you'll find exactly—"

"Stop!" the cop commanded both. "We'll sort it out at the precinct. You're with me, sir."

Matt nodded regally. "I am appreciative, officer."

Zachery nodded. "I'll ride along with you, so—"

"Against regs. Grab a cab. Meet us at 233 West Tenth."

"Certainly," Zachery acquiesced, masking annoyance. "And police in Sleepy Hollow are likely looking for him."

"We'll check. Get it squared away."

"Happy to help, officer. I'll meet you there." As the cop turned Matt to go, Zachery whispered into his ear, "I'll kiss Molly for you later."

Matt flared slightly, but the cop hung on to his bony arm. "Hey. Take it easy, Gramps. I don't wanna cuff you."

The policeman led him down the sidewalk. Zachery sucked some air through his teeth with annoyance as he watched the slouching remnants of his dying body being led away, then looked for a taxi.

~~~~

ON EAST NINTH STREET A FEW MOMENTS LATER, THE OFFICER was walking beside the old man, who appeared listless. But Matt wasn't. His alert eyes were scanning for any opportunity while the cop was preoccupied on his radio earbud. "Yes…Sleepy Hollow. Near Tarrytown… Yeah… Check their PD."

Just ahead Matt spotted a messenger pausing his electric scooter by the curb to buy a soda from a sidewalk vendor as the cop continued, "Right: elderly mixed-race male, about eighty and—*Hey!*"

Matt had bolted sideways from the cop. He shoved the messenger off the scooter, which he commandeered and zipped away, full-throttle. The cop fumbled with his radio as the messenger yelled profanities.

On the scooter, Matt was breathing hard with nervous tension, but maneuvering the scooter with inherent dexterity. He weaved quickly—dangerously—through moving cars and vehicles that battled for their way. His trench coat billowed out behind him like Batman's cape.

Numerous pedestrians saw and laughed or applauded. Three street teens cheered the old geezer flying by, shouting to him, "Yeah! Go, Pops! You got skills, dude!"

Matt felt a wonderful rush at finally being in control of the moment.

He crossed Sixth Avenue, driving flat out. But as he veered left to go south on Christopher, he was stabbed with chest pain. The scooter bobbled, nearly hitting a woman; Matt barely regained control, but was losing confidence. He angled the scooter in between two parked cars and stopped.

Matt stood there leaning on a car, huffing and puffing, struggling to control his breathing. As the elation of the scooter ride slipped away, he again faced crushing reality. He went into a corner market to fetch a bottle of water. At the counter he fished out his wallet—only two dollars left. He decided using Zachery's card at this point wouldn't matter. He handed the Platinum Amex to the heavily tattooed cashier, who was reading *Vanity Fair*.

The cashier scanned it, said, "Card's no good."

"What?"

"You need cash. Four bucks. Card's cancelled."

Matt realized, *Of course.* Zachery would have cancelled all his cards by now.

He emerged from the store into the freezing afternoon, without any water. He walked disconsolately south on West Fourth, feeling claustrophobic. Zachery seemed to have anticipated his every move, closed off all possible avenues of help. He had painted Matt into an ever-narrowing corner.

Then Matt realized that his hand was clenching the lower pocket he had zippered closed on his cargo shirt. He took out the talisman, tried again to remember, "'*Awat ah-lone...Awat...*' Oh shit."

He sagged. With no idea of the ancient phrase, or even if it would work again, he was tempted to throw the relic in a trash can, but didn't. He pocketed it, leaned against a mailbox, near tears of hopelessness. He noticed the hated reflection of himself in a store window. He glanced away sourly.

But then Matt paused, and looked back carefully at Zachery's reflection.

Matt was remembering how he'd first met the old man.

Chapter 11

The late afternoon sun shined in through the windows of the high-end, NYU executive office. Elegant, distinguished Dean William Sanger was personally ushering in his prestigious old friend Dr. John Zachery. "Don't be ridiculous, John. You could never impose. A man with your credentials? Your esteem?" Sanger eased the heavy walnut office door closed, then with a private smile added confidentially, "Your amazing ability to procure wild women?"

Matt nearly choked. He tried to nod and smile back as Dean Sanger opened a beautiful inlaid cabinet and extracted a crystal decanter of Chivas, speaking with fond remembrance, "I'm still recovering from those two Frenchies you snagged for us at the Met exhibit last year."

"Yes," Matt was trying to ignore his nerves, vamping, "That was...certainly qu-quite an experience—" he almost said "sir" but caught himself—"Willy."

"And so damned convenient." Sanger grinned. "With your townhouse just up there on Eighty-Eighth."

Matt was intent, processing. "...Right."

The dean poured two fingers of Scotch into a couple glasses. "What'd you pay for that place? And smack against the goddamn Guggenheim! Jesus!"

"Well, you know." Matt said modestly, "A few g-good antiquity sales—"

"Good?" Sanger guffawed. "More like you cornered the market and fleeced the billionaires, you old cutthroat." He handed his old comrade a glass and clinked it. "Chin chin." He took a big sip.

Matt faked it, just wetting his lips, as Sanger waved him to the rich leather couch and sat opposite, continuing, "Not that I'm complaining, John-boy. You sure helped me make a few bucks. And got me *that* beauty." Matt looked where Sanger was pointing and found himself being stared at by the androgynous stone face of a very peculiar "angel" from Chartres Cathedral. Her/His/Its bizarre, giddy smile/gaze was surprisingly lifelike and oddly unsettling, as though seeing through his subterfuge.

"Got me other great pieces, including more than a few young ladies, huh?" Sanger laughed licentiously. Matt forced a companionable laugh. Sanger looked toward the ceiling with a fond sigh. "But those two Parisian nymphs. *Tres formidable!*" He leaned toward his friend's graying head, speaking very *entre nous,* "Remember the way that blond could wrap her—"

"Do I ever!" Matt interrupted good-naturedly, setting his glass aside. "But listen, Willy, I'd like your thoughts about something." He took out the talisman, passed it to Sanger. "What do you m-make of that?"

Matt was privately amused to see Sanger put on the eyeglasses he'd avoided using at the alumni gathering.

"Hmmm." Sanger turned it over in his manicured fingers. "Interesting piece. Post-Roman Celtic, of course."

Matt was surprised. "Not Sumerian?"

"No," Dean Sanger chortled as though his old colleague was joking. "And not from Coney Island either. Early Middle Ages, huh?"

"Tell me your opinion, W-Willy."

"Oh, you're more expert in that period." He smiled warmly. "I always loved that passage in your first book: 'That time in English history veiled in shadowy mystery.' And also: 'Those days of alchemists and sorcerers and witchery.' You should've been a damned songwriter."

As Sanger picked up a magnifying glass, Matt asked, "And the head with two faces?"

"Janus, obviously. Roman god of beginnings—whence we get January." Matt nodded as Sanger continued, "But also god of many other things: gates, transitions, passages and—of course—*duality*." Sanger drew a breath. "Yes. I'd put it about four or five hundred AD. The tiny sharp prongs are curious. Seems like some sort of ritual piece."

"Certainly a possibility," Matt said quietly, thinking, *If only you knew, Willy-boy.*

Sanger strained to inspect a detail more closely. He picked up a smaller, thicker magnifier, scrutinizing a tiny detail as Matt prodded, "Any ideas about the metaphysics of it?"

Sanger brought the talisman and magnifier to within an inch of his eye. "Well, metaphysics are definitely out of my line so—" A look of astonishment suddenly flooded Sanger's face, leaving him speechless. He glanced up with a grin. "You sly old bastard! You've been baiting me. Waiting to see my reaction."

Matt's heart rate increased, but he stayed calm, let it play, also raised a cocksure eyebrow encouraging Sanger to continue.

The dean looked again through the high-power magnifier. "I've never seen such a tiny engraving of it, but it's clearly the winged lion with eagle claws. The symbol associated with England's legendary *Uther Pendragon!*"

Matt did his best to nod smugly, awaiting more details, but saw Sanger turn pale, suddenly fearful about what he was holding, staring at the talisman with an awestruck—almost frightened—expression. "Jesus, John!" His voice became a very nervous whisper. "Do you realize what you have here?!"

Matt pretended to challenge Sanger. "Tell me, Willy."

"This could be something that belonged to—or was even *created by*—Merlin!"

Matt felt a ton of bricks fall onto him. But he remained dead calm. Showed no reaction. Forced his eyes to hold steadily on Sanger despite Matt's insides churning like an EF-5 tornado. He said with quiet humor, "Yes. Well. That would explain a lot."

Sanger glanced at him, "About what?"

"Oh, just," Matt shrugged, his voice totally level, "certain s-suspicions, ideas I've had."

Sanger carefully—almost reverently—passed the talisman back to his aged colleague. "Oh, I get it, you cagey old SOB. You're planning another book."

Matt smiled. "Possibly."

A few minutes later Dean Sanger was walking his old friend to the elevator. "Truly a historic find, John. An astounding piece." He whispered confidentially, "The Smithsonian—or definitely the Getty—will pay a fortune for it. I'm honored that you let me in on your marvelous secret."

Matt couldn't resist. "Well, at least *one* of my secrets." His eyes twinkled.

"You bugger." Sanger clapped his colleague's shoulder. "I can't believe how you played me."

"You were a good sport, Willy." Matt chuckled, having thus been handed another idea to parlay. "And by the way," he whispered, "this is em-embarrassing to ask, but I had a senior moment today and I'm running a little short of cash, do you think I could possibly—"

"Anything for you, John-boy!" Sanger opened his Gucci wallet wide. "Whatever you need."

Matt gladly took a healthy pinch of bills and momentarily forgot himself, saying, "Thanks, man. You rock!"

Sanger laughed heartily as the elevator door opened. "And *you* sound like a student!"

Sanger's wrinkled old pal stepped into the elevator then glanced back through his wireframe glasses chuckling. "Wish I looked like one!"

They shared a comradely laugh as the elevator door closed.

~~~~

THE NYPD SIXTH PRECINCT BOOKING AREA WAS BUSY WITH noisy civilians, lawyers and cops escorting perpetrators in or away in cuffs. The Duty Officer behind her tall desk was searching her digital records. She shook her head at the young, frustrated collegiate guy facing her as Zachery snapped, "But the officer told me to meet him here."

"What can I say? No John Zachery got logged in today at this, or any, station. Sorry." She looked past him, "Next."

Zachery turned away in a frustrated huff.

~~~~

IN THE MED-X LAB, DEV WAS INPUTTING PATHOLOGICAL analysis data into a computer while answering his ringing desk phone. "Bhandari, Lab One."

A voice whispered, "Hey, Dev. It's Matt."

Dev frowned at the caller ID. "What's this number?"

Matt was on a cell outside the Alumni Building. "It's a throwaway I just bought." *Thank you, Willy,* Matt thought. He continued whispering so Dev won't hear his basso voice, "My number got hacked. Don't call or text that one."

"Okay, but what's with your voice? Too many cigars today?"

"Cigars?"

"Yes. I was greatly astonished to see you puffing that Godzilla stogie in the square today." Dev kept entering pathology data as he talked. "Could not believe it was you."

With a chill, Matt realized Dev must have encountered Zachery. "Well," Matt whispered grimly, "I h-haven't been myself lately." He wanted to hear more about the imposter, but stayed on course. "And I've got a sore throat. But listen, Dev, if I wanted to check out the metaphysics of an ancient relic, who would I talk to?"

"Excuse me?!" Dev stopped typing, sat bolt upright. "I cannot believe that I am talking to Matthew Shaw. Is this really Mr. I-don't-believe-anything-I-can't-verify talking about *metaphysics!?* Since when?"

"Just this morning, actually. I decided to have a more open mind."

Dev looked heavenward with arms stretched up. "Thank you, Nostradamus!"

Then he opened Google. "What kind of a relic?"

"An ancient Celtic talisman."

"Way cool!" He was typing in parameters.

"So who knows about that kind of—"

"Thelma Greer, duh," Dev stated the obvious. "And if she doesn't, she'll know who does. You should have heard her speak at the convention, Mattsy." He was typing and clicking continuously. "About her years at Duke studying paranormal stuff. Then how she ran the Parapsych Unit at UCLA. Claimed they dumped her when her books got a little too far-out for academia. But she the man. Uh, wo-man."

"Got any idea where I could—"

"Checking her site." A photo of Thelma's sixtyish face with

tinted glasses appeared on his screen. She looked keenly intelligent. Dev checked details, saying, "Hey, I'm doing the convention again tonight. Swapped out my evening shift for a red-eye here till six AM, so don't wait up." He squinted at his screen. "Hmm, she mentioned living in the city, but there's only an e-mail address."

"Then write her for me, will you? Tell her it's urgent. Set an appointment for me right away. I don't trust my regular email so use my Med-X address or call this number."

"Okay," Dev said energetically, "chances of getting a reply are slim, since she's like the Dali Lama of this shit. But if you meet her up close, I get to be with you!"

Matt sighed. "That would definitely be an eye-opening experience for you."

~~~~

PACING RESTLESSLY AROUND THE EMPTY FOUNTAIN BENEATH winter-barren trees in Father Demo Square on Bleeker, an annoyed Zachery massaged the knot in his stomach. It was near dusk. He listened angrily on Matt's cell for the seventeenth time as a cheerful AI voice said, "If you're inquiring about a JPMorgan Chase account, press two." He did, listened expectantly, then heard yet again, "We're sorry, but due to a system-wide computer malfunction, that option is not available at this time. To return to the main—"

Zachery slapped the phone. Almost threw it in a trash can. He stood steaming, took a deep breath, trying unsuccessfully to be calm. His fingers dug out the small pack of Tums and he chewed two of them as he rubbed his stomach. Then he sensed someone watching him and glanced up sharply. It was friendly-faced Antonio Demo, or rather a bronze, life-size statue of the 1935 pastor of neighboring Our Lady of Pompei Church. The priest's beneficent eyes seemed focused on Zachery, offering comfort.

Zachery snorted with irritation and turned away.

~~~~

SEEN THROUGH THE WINDOWS OF A BARNES & NOBLE, twilight was settling on Lower Broadway as Matt moved among browsing patrons. He was unsteady again, a pressing reminder that his body was weakening. He found a hardback titled *Beyond* by Thelma Greer. She stared out from the cover with her frizzy hair and no-nonsense look. Matt opened to the copyright page.

Moments later, he was sitting on a stool between bookshelves with the cell to his ear. He'd worked his way through the Random House phone menu to a fatigued female near the end of her day.

"Hello. Denise Pingatore."

"Ms. Pingatore, hi," Matt said pleasantly, "I'm delighted to reach you."

She was uncaring. "What do you need?"

"You're the editor for Thelma Greer, is that—"

"I *was*, yes." A sour memory.

"Well I really need to get in touch with her about an important—"

"You can write to her in care of us. We're at—"

"No, no. I have to talk to her *immediately*. She's the only one who—"

"I'm sorry, sir, but I can't give out any—"

"Ms. Pingatore," Matt said authoritatively, puffing up, "my name is Dr. John Zachery, I'm a fellow published author and—"

"That may be, sir. But you have no idea the number of people who want to talk to Ms. Greer 'immediately.' Just stay on the line, you'll hear our address." She clicked off and an automated voice began providing it.

Matt hung up, perturbed but determined. He was sitting in the Biography section. He stood and looked for History.

He went to the alphabetical end of that one and under Z he found *From England to America* with his current face on the back cover. He flipped to the acknowledgements page, then heard an astonished male voice. "Oh my God! It's him! You're you!"

Matt glanced through his wireframes at the trim, fastidious thirty-something, juggling his grande cappuccino, eager to shake hands.

"Dr. Zachery, right?!"

"Uh...yes." Matt said, mildly amused. "I have been all day, actually."

The guy laughed, shook his hand, gushing, "I can't believe it! I'm—my partner and I are huuuuge fans of your work. Could you —would you mind autographing a copy for us?"

Matt blinked, smiled wanly, and did so.

<center>~~~~</center>

THE MANHATTAN SKYLINE WITH LIGHTS TWINKLING IN THE gathering darkness could be seen out the window of a different editor's small office. Several books on her shelves were by Zachery. A sprightly, Chinese-American woman in her forties with irresistible warmth answered her phone. "Hi, this is Jessica Lee."

Matt took the plunge, "Hi, Jessica, this is—"

"Dr. Zachery, of course!" Jessica was all smiles. "I'd know that majestic voice anywhere. How *are* you!"

"Fine, fine," Matt was relieved by her response. "Not quite as y-young as I used to be but surviving."

"I'm really glad to hear that, sir."

"And let me thank you again, Jessica, for all the really cool—I mean all your truly w-wonderful work on *From England to America* and the other books."

"Oh, please, it's my honor." She laughed lightly. "And 'really cool' from you is the best praise ever."

"Good to know." Matt smiled, then spoke more confidentially. "Listen Jessica, I need help getting in touch with a fellow author. Maybe even have you make an introductory call for me?"

"Absolutely!" Jessica grabbed a pen, enthusiastic to do whatever she could. "Shoot."

~~~~

ZACHERY WAS FROWNING AS HE WALKED ALONG COLD, shadowy Bleeker, a few blocks from Matt's apartment building. He was still disgruntled over JPMorgan Chase's ongoing computer glitch when a voice called out, "Yo! Mattsy!"

Zachery saw Dev just climbing onto a bus, shouting, "I'm headed back to the convention. No word yet from Thelma Greer about your relic. But maybe I can ask her when she's there tomorrow. See ya!"

The bus rolled away. Zachery watched, his own wheels turning.

~~~~

NIGHT HAD FULLY FALLEN BY THE TIME MATT TURNED THE corner from Central Park West onto West Eighty-Second Street, just north of the Natural History Museum. An ice-cold wind off the Hudson was stinging his craggy face. He coughed as he went up the weathered stone front steps toward the entrance of the four-story brownstone at number seven, the address Jessica Lee had scored for him. He pushed the buzzer.

The door had two narrow panels of beveled glass which divided and multiplied the image of the woman approaching on the inside, somewhat Picasso-like, Matt thought. But he had no difficulty recognizing the face of Thelma Greer. She appeared slightly older than on the posters and book covers. Her frizzy hair was sprinkled with gray, but her businesslike demeanor and sharp eyes behind her slightly tinted glasses connoted strength. Also frowning suspicion.

She moved her head slightly side to side to get an optimum view through the bifurcating window glass of the old Anglo-Black gentleman with a moustache, beard, and knit cap. She was brusque. "What do you want?"

"Dr. Greer? I'm Dr. J-John Zachery. Author of many history volumes. I think my publisher called you to—"

"Haven't checked my messages. What do you want?"

"I've had a bizarre experience and—"

"Haven't we all. Put it in a letter and I'll—"

"No, please! This is a m-matter of—"

"Life and death. I'm sure. In a letter, pal. Sorry, but—"

"You oughta let them in, Thel," said a strange, raspy voice behind her.

Greer said back over her shoulder, "I'll handle it, Skeeter. And it's not a 'them.' There's only one."

Matt saw a wiry black man limp up just behind Greer's shoulder. He was sightless, his eyes merely blue-white membranes. His face was horribly disfigured from burns, his scarred head had only a few patches of hair, and his lips were almost nonexistent. His image was all the more unnerving seen through the multiple cut-glass angles. But his hoarse voice was confident as he said emphatically, "No Thel—they's *two*."

Skeeter smiled strangely. Which amplified his ghastly appearance. Greer studied Skeeter's expression as Matt drew a hopeful breath.

Then he heard the door being unlocked.

~~~~

In the Sleepy Hollow mansion's Vanderbilt-sized kitchen, Jamison was on the phone, frowning. "No, Mr. Shaw, we've not yet located Dr. Zachery. Heard nothing about the NYPD holding him or that scene you described at NYU. It's all very disturbing."

"Yes, it is," Zachery snapped, thinking, *on several levels.* He was on his cell, having stopped into a coffee shop at the corner of Bleeker and Bank across from Matt's four-story, red-brick building. "Please call me if you hear anything."

When the call ended, Zachery sat pondering, unmindful of the evening traffic and passing pedestrians. He unconsciously pulled his lower lip as his youthful eyes narrowed and he tried to piece together what was going on.

~~~~

Matt was sitting on a 1920s red velvet settee in Thelma Greer's drawing room, which featured mostly Art Deco furniture, real Tiffany lamps with their multitudinous leaded glass colors and *objets d'art* of the same period. But there was also a healthy sprinkling of intriguing items such as Matt had once seen in the old Times Square *Ripley's Believe It or Not Museum.* Here a shrunken head, there a framed nude photo of 1890s conjoined twins, elsewhere a handmade voodoo doll, complete with pins, inside a bell jar on an end table.

Dev would be absolutely freaking about all of this, Matt thought. He was watching the totally blind man pouring steaming hot tea into a fine china cup and instinctively stopping at the perfect moment the cup was full. Then the man set down the teapot on the low coffee table between them, and in his hoarse, raspy voice he asked Matt, "Sweetener?"

"Uh, no. Thanks, M-Mister—"

"Jus' plain ol' Skeeter, son."

Matt glanced at the other end table, seeing a framed photo of Thelma with a middle-aged man and older woman.

Skeeter instantly said, "That be Thel's brother, name of Max. Lives with their momma up in Albany."

"Ah." Then Matt asked quietly, "Excuse me, but h-how'd you know I was looking at—"

"You be surprised all the shit I can see nowadays...Matthew."

Skeeter wiggled his hairless eyebrows and limped confidently toward the large kitchen, instinctively navigating the obstacle course around a sleeping calico cat, then a leather ottoman, then gracefully avoiding collision with preoccupied Dr. Greer.

Barely five feet tall, she wore an intricately embroidered, navy-blue silk kimono. She'd been pacing slowly around her eclectic, somewhat spooky parlor. Her brow was pinched thoughtfully as she studied Matt's talisman.

Then she stood directly in front of him, with a serious, no-nonsense attitude, clicked a digital recorder and delivered what was apparently her standard full disclosure. "You understand that I, Dr. Thelma Moss, document and copyright all aspects of my investigations. Including everything you say here. Is that agreeable to you, Matthew Shaw, now apparently inhabiting the physical body of Dr. John Zachery?"

"Y-yes. I agree. Um…is Skeeter a psychic?"

"Among other things." She sat at her desk, donning a pair of jeweler's glasses with multiple lenses. "Ever since his career as a pimp abruptly ended seventeen years ago."

"H-How did he—?"

"He was burned and blinded in some kind of spontaneous combustion phenomenon. One of his whores exploded into flames while he was beating her up and—"

"Wait. 'Exploded into—'"

"That's right, Matthew. There's nineteen million people in this goddamn city. You think yours is the only paranormal occurrence going on?" She raised her eyebrows at him pointedly, then she flipped a magnifier, examining the talisman more closely.

Matt glanced from her to Skeeter. For the first time, he was feeling hopeful.

~~~~

At the Bleeker flat's worktable, Zachery's young fingers typed quickly. A mouse click brought images of Dr. Greer onto the laptop's screen along with a long bio and book covers. Zachery inhaled with satisfaction that his instincts had been correct.

Then he continued typing, searching deeper.

Chapter 12

The well-fed, raven-black cat named Luna was enjoying the strokes of Matt's long, old fingers. She was lounging near Dr. Greer's monitor, atop which was an A/V camera. Matt watched the screen as Thelma scrolled through images of artifacts similar to the talisman. Skeeter sat nearby, listening.

"It's definitely from this style of relic, Matt. Early Dark Ages."

"And connected to Merlin or black magic or—?"

"Well, *some* kind of alchemy. Your vision of Stonehenge suggests Druidic origins. We'll check my databases for that trigger phrase. And all you remember is…?"

"'*Awat-ah-lone…*' That's only about half of it. So frustrating."

Her screen shifted to scroll medieval illuminated manuscripts. "He used salt and water?"

Matt nodded, unconsciously rubbing his hand over his cropped hair, and reacting to its texture. "God. I keep expecting to feel *my own* hair!"

Thelma paused, focused on him with sincere sympathy. "I can only imagine how awful it must be, Matt."

"Dev said you'd be about the only person in the world who *could* imagine it. I'm r-really, really grateful, y'know?"

"I do know." Thelma smiled encouragingly. "And let me tell you, Matt, your startling situation is uniquely terrible because you're the real deal, you *actually are* inhabiting a body that isn't yours. But you're not alone when it comes to those feelings." She saw his confusion and continued empathetically. "What you're feeling; I often feel myself. Watching the face in my mirror sneaking in wrinkles, decomposing slightly every day, knowing damn well I'm seventy-six and time is not my friend. Which all seems completely crazy because *I still feel like a freshman at Yale!* That's how I *feel.* And millions of us golden oldies feel the same way."

"That's the only good thing 'bout being blind," Skeeter rasped. "Don't have to see no old geezer reflection lookin' back at me."

"Aye, Skeeter, there's the annoying rub." Thelma agreed, then smiled at Matt. "My crackerjack Gramma used to quote an old baseball player, Satchel Paige, who said, 'How old would you be if you didn't know how old you was?' And on the very day Gramma died—at a hundred and one—she told me that *she still felt like a teenager.* Her counsel to me had always been to live like she had: to savor and appreciate every, every day *while she lived it...every moment.*"

"*Carpe diem.*" Matt nodded, sighing. "I've al-always tried to do that, Thelma, but—"

"But now you're trapped. Yes. Inside an impossible metaphysical nightmare with no exit." Her voice became deep and foreboding, "'*Which offers you this chilling challenge—*'"

Matt chuckled, recognized she was channeling Disney's Haunted Mansion. He completed the dramatic quote, "'...*To find a way out!'* Yes. The reason I c-came to you."

Thelma smiled, squeezed his frail arm. "And we're going to do that, boyo." She looked at her computer screen. "So. The salt. That likely keyed the transmigration to sunrise."

"You mean if he hadn't used salt—"

"It probably would've happened instantaneously."

"And he didn't want me to freak in the r-restaurant. Duh."

"But despite the salt, a measure of migration obviously began."

"Because of the visions I had, yeah: the helicopter pad, that airborne point of view. I was already getting glimpses through Zachery's eyes." Matt was trying to get his head around it. "So, then the lecture hall, his college students liking 'me,' the man on Houston Street fighting 'me.' They were Zachery's *memories?*"

"Seems likely."

"But what about the *older* stuff I saw? The Nazi dirigible, that slave ship? Witch trials? Stonehenge?"

"Likely also memories, because Zachery's body—and yours—certainly weren't the first to be occupied by…whatever the Entity is."

"Thas right." Skeeter nodded. "He gotta be an *old* muthafucka."

They glanced at Skeeter. "And clearly on the Dark Side," Thelma confirmed, "using Merlin-level power to take over dozens of lives like yours, Matt. Across the centuries. Plus engaging in nefarious, diabolical enterprises for its own gain. Or twisted pleasure."

Matt weighed it all. "Dev said you'd 'seen some weird, scary shit,' but anything like—"

"Close." She mused. "Close. But *this*…is exceedingly challenging." She was looking inward, deeply. "*Defeating it*, however, now that could be an important service."

"Not just to me. Also, to whoever's his next victim. And on and on."

"Right. And we already have a head start: We've got one of the Ruby Slippers."

Matt's wrinkled brow knitted, "Wh-what?"

"Dorothy had the pair of them. They were the secret key that would get her back home. You remember half of that trigger phrase that could help you escape. We just need to find the other half."

Matt understood. "The other 'Ruby Slipper.'"

"Exactly." Then Thelma inhaled deeply, her countenance became more serious than he had yet seen. "But it requires going deeper, under hypnosis, with you possibly facing serious discomfort. I can't in good conscience urge you to—"

"No urging needed," he said immediately. "Last year, Dev showed me that article in *Rolling Stone* about you using hypnosis in research. And if there's a chance we could—"

"Before you talk yourself into anything, Matt, listen to me: there's cognitive danger involved, a possibility you might not come out feeling entirely—"

He held up his age-spotted, wrinkled hands, palms toward her. Their eyes locked on each other. Then she nodded appreciation of his bravery, determination, and acceptance of the challenge.

~~~~

Using her skills as a hypnotherapist, Dr. Greer had taken Matt deeply under in less than thirty minutes. He was sitting in a comfortable, high-backed chair, eyes closed, with Thelma and Skeeter nearby. Her voice was warm, soothing, confidence-inspiring.

"You're entirely relaxed and completely safe, Matt." She took a breath. "Now we're going to work our way back to the night of the dinner. Let's start in your apartment. You were sleeping restlessly…?

"Yes," Matt said in a low monotone. "Dreaming…like that college lecture hall. I was at a podium, students laughed. They liked me."

"Zachery's a popular lecturer. What else did you dream about?"

"Flying aboard the Concorde…"

Thelma considered, "Okay, late 1960s. Before you were born."

"Then it got weirder…the 1930s Prohibition gangsters. The 1899 funeral at Old Trinity Church… I felt like I knew who was being buried. Then the slave ship where I felt I was captain. It was awful. But also, I felt this weird rush." His eyes remained closed as he frowned. "Like...like when I watched that French girl being burned at the stake."

She saw Matt tensing up.

"Easy. You're an objective observer now."

He relaxed slightly, eyes still closed. "I was the one who'd condemned her. And..."

Dr. Greer saw Matt's wrinkled hand push down on his crotch. "And what?"

The old man's face fluctuated between revulsion and delight, Matt's deep voice sounding embarrassed. "Seeing her burn gave me...an e-erection... Triggered flashes of sex...with lots of different women. A medieval farm girl. An Austrian duchess with a beauty mark on her chin...in a room at Versailles...under construction."

Greer whispered, "Mid-1600s?"

"Yes. I felt lust... Some women were enjoying it, but many others were fighting against me—against *him*... Like the shadowy blond...struggling against being raped... The walls beside her are pulsating...oh. It's a tent."

"A tent?"

"For camping. It's windy outside. And campfire light. Feels like a desert."

"Go on, Matt, dig deeper and—"

"Dig! Yes!"

"What?" Thelma was confused.

"It's at a 'dig.' Archeological."

"Where?"

Matt's closed eyes squinted tighter, his mind probing. "... maybe M-Maktar?"

Thelma's encyclopedic brain searched for it. "I think that's Tunisia."

"She's struggling...my—*Zachery's*—hand is covering her mouth...tightly...her hand's on top now...clawing at his...frantically…she has a wedding ring…it's—" he choked, whispered—"my mother's!" Matt's body quaked. His face clenched, horrified.

Thelma spoke soothingly, "Easy, Matt…stay objective, just an observer."

His shuddering subsided, but he remained tense. He whispered, "That memory seems…related to the night on Houston Street…"

"Where the man attacked you? Can you see him now?" Thelma saw rapid eye movement under Matt's closed lids.

"It's jumbled light and shadows…there's a sign behind him. It's 1999 and—ouch!" Matt flinched, ducked his head. "The man is hitting my face…angry… In and out of the light… He's… ohmigod. He's…"

"Who?" Thelma asked and the response came from Skeeter and Matt simultaneously:

"His poppa."

"My father."

Thelma glanced at Skeeter's membranous eyes. He nodded confirmation. Then she asked Matt, "Why is he attacking you?"

"He's furious at me about something… I'm grabbing his collar. I see headlights coming. A car. Speeding. Perfect!" Matt smiled gleefully, thrusting out both hands. "Ha! I threw him in f-front of the car! Good riddance!" Matt laughed, triumphant—then was aghast.

Thelma leaned closer. "What happened?"

"It's what killed my father! Not a hit-and-run accident! I did it."

"Not you, Matt. It was—"

"Zachery!" Matt's eyes snapped open. But stared blankly. Thelma saw he was still in the trance, breathing hard, dry-mouthed.

"Easy now, Matt." Thelma was shaken, but stayed in control. "Let your eyes close again. That's it, good. Except for today, the rest all happened before you were born. There was nothing you could have done." His breathing normalized. "That's better. Now let's get to your dinner with Zachery. Can you see the restaurant?"

"Yes," Matt murmured. "I'm at the table. He's sprinkling salt…a drop of water… He's pressing the talisman into my hand—ouch! It stings!"

"Good. Now listen carefully…"

Matt squinted, focusing on the moment. "Zachery says, '*Awat ah-lone sin yah, tahm walla tey—*'"

Matt recoiled, electrified. He gasped. His eyes snapped open, fully awake, disoriented. Thelma rested her hand on his arm. "It's okay. What happened?"

"It w-was…like lightning. A flash of that one-eyed man at Stonehenge, then for an instant I was looking through Zachery's eyes at myself!" He blinked. "But did you hear the phrase?"

Skeeter held up Thelma's digital recorder indicating he'd captured it. Then he hoarsely recited, *"Awat ah-lone sin yah, tahm walla tey.'"*

"Yes!" Matt was elated. "Yes, that was—no. No wait. There's another word. I saw Zachery's lips moving."

Skeeter shook his head. "That's all you said, buds."

Matt was annoyed. "Shit! The jolt covered it up."

"That's okay." Thelma patted his arm. "You did great, Matt. We got a big piece. And if you're still game—"

"Absolutely!"

Moments later, Matt was deep under hypnosis again, back at the posh table in Moonshadows.

Thelma and Skeeter leaned nearer to Matt sitting in the chair, eyes closed, concentrating hard. "Ouch! It stings… Zachery says, '*Awat ah-lone sin yah, tahm walla tey—*'"

The lightning crack jolted Matt awake. Gasping, he looked eagerly at Thelma and Skeeter whose expressions were negative.

Skeeter whispered, "Sorry, buds."

Matt sagged under the weight of disappointment.

Thelma was already moving to her computer. "We'll figure it out, Matt. You've given us lots to go on. I just need a little time with Hal here."

"And I could dig deeper into Zachery." Matt glanced around. "You have another computer?"

"Not working right now."

"Where's the nearest cybercafé?"

"Best one's straight down at Columbus Circle."

"Okay. Maybe something about him or in one of his b-books might help us." He scribbled on a Post-it. "Here's my Med-X lab e-mail if you find anything." He grabbed Zachery's overcoat. "And we all agree he's d-done this before, huh?"

"Assuredly." Thelma said, already typing.

"Stayin' alive's the primo instinct, son," Skeeter rasped, then postulated, "Be mighty easy to get hooked on this kinda shit. Be tempted to try it myself. Who wouldn't want to, s'pecially if y'could stay young, powerful, and rich forever?"

Matt considered that as Thelma chimed in, while typing at light-speed, "And it was your own survival instinct, boyo, that brought you to us. Plus, a huge dose of bravery, determination."

Matt felt overwhelmed by having two such potent compatriots. "Listen, I...I don't know how to e-even begin to—"

"Hey." Thelma stopped typing, looked at him serenely. Her warm expression conveyed her world of understanding and sympathetic feelings for him. Matt nodded appreciation. Skeeter blindly held out his hand for a slap, which Matt gratefully delivered as he hurried out.

~~~~

THE COLUMBUS CIRCLE COMPUTER CAFE WAS NICELY appointed and trendy. A friendly young Samoan picked up the empty coffee mug beside the old man with the moustache and Van Dyke beard and asked if he'd like another. Matt smiled, declined.

Wearing earbuds, he was on Zoom with Thelma, seen in a small window at the screen's corner. Other textual information filled the rest.

"I'm not sure any of this will help, but it's an eye-opener," Matt said. "We know in the mid-1960s, Zachery was about my age and received his huge inheritance."

"From that rum-runner guy." Thelma nodded. "Costanza."

"Right. But get this." He highlighted a line onscreen. "Costanza had received a big inheritance when *he* was twenty in 1899! Came from an aging New York robber-baron named McClain, who was buried that year at—"

"Old Trinity Church." Thelma deduced.

"Yes. And McClain had been a twenty-something sailor in the 1840s when *he* came into a fortune from a slave-trader named Fredericks." Matt coughed. "And that's only as far back as I've traced."

"You felt your Stonehenge vision was 503 AD. That's quite a run, boyo."

"But why me this time?"

Thelma pondered. "Just 'lucky'? But listen, I think I'm closing in on that last word."

"Oh my God, really?" Matt felt energized. "Okay, I'll check a couple more things, then head back up."

~~~~

SOON THEREAFTER, THELMA WAS WORKING AT HER COMPUTER when her door buzzer sounded. She called over her shoulder, "Skeeter? I'm right in the middle of—"

"Yeah," Skeeter said from the kitchen, "I got it, Thel."

As Skeeter limped out through her study toward the front door his head tilted up slightly, like a dog sensing something pleasant. He smiled. "It's just 'them' again."

Thelma was distracted by what was on her screen. "Who? I'll be there in a sec."

Skeeter opened the front door, unable to see that it was the other 'them.'

A young man in a skimpy windbreaker, jeans, plus gloves and a knit cap was facing away.

Skeeter smiled blindly. "Welcome back."

As Zachery turned, he pulled the front of his cap down to become a ski mask, saying, "Thank you."

~~~~

THE ANGELIC MARBLE STATUES ATOP THE COLUMBUS CIRCLE monument solemnly watched an uptown bus passing on rainy Central Park West. Inside the bus, eighty-year-old Matt was looking up at the statues. He had climbed aboard when he left the computer café into light rain and no available taxis.

He noticed a young Hispanic couple on the bus nuzzling each other sweetly.

An eightyish woman across the aisle from Matt also saw them, grinned at him. "Seems like yesterday, huh? When we were like that?"

Matt sighed. "Seems *exactly* like yesterday."

"Funny thing is, I still feel the same on the inside, don't you?"

"Yes, ma'am." Matt weighed that as he looked at the faces of several older people, seeing them differently than he would have previously, realizing how precious life was, how he'd never appreciated every moment while he was living it until that day. He coughed, raspier. He knew the grains of sand in his hourglass were slipping away.

At the Natural History Museum, he got off, hurried up Central Park West, hoping Thelma had made headway. The rain had turned to sleet. Approaching the corner at Eighty-Second he slowed, seeing flashing lights of multiple police cars. Edging closer he saw uniformed officers going in and out of Thelma's door.

Matt ducked back, worried.

Inside Thelma's drawing room, her phone rang. A rookie police-woman wearing blue nitrile gloves glanced at a plainclothes detective for permission. He nodded. She lifted the receiver. "Yes, hello?"

She heard a man's bass voice, "May I speak to Thelma, please?"

The rookie covered the mouthpiece, whispering to the detective, "Male, deep voice." He signaled her to continue. "Who's calling?"

Matt was around the corner on his throwaway cell, troubled. "This is…her brother, M-Max Greer. Who are you?"

"NYPD, Mr. Greer."

Matt's throat tightened. "Is something wrong?"

"Can you come here to her house?"

"I'm…out of town. In…" he hedged, "Chicago. Is Thelma alright?"

"You're her brother, sir?"

Matt could barely whisper, "Yes."

The rookie swallowed. This was a first for her. She spoke gently, "I'm afraid there's no easy way to say this, sir… Your sister's no longer alive."

"What?!" Matt's heart clutched.

The rookie was striving to stay professional. "I'm so very sorry, Mr. Greer. There was a second victim also. An older man. African-American. With old burn scars. We don't have an ID yet, but—"

"Oh, God." Matt was choking, lost. "Th-this is…how did you find out?"

"We got an anonymous tip. Someone saw a lone, elderly man entering, heard a disturbance and—"

"Wait. 'Elderly'...?"

"Yes, sir."

"Do you have any idea who it—?"

"We're dusting for prints now."

Matt inhaled sharply, glanced down at his fingertips. Tried to think. Then said shakily, "Can you...can you w-withhold any public statements until I've told our mother?"

"I think so, sir. But did your sister ever mention a Dr. John Zachery?"

"Uh, n-no," he stammered, feeling cold sweat. "Why?"

"In her office trash can we found a note he'd apparently sent. Threatening Dr. Greer. We've found some photos of Zachery online. We'll find him, sir... Sir?" She looked at the detective. "He hung up."

Standing on the sidewalk, Matt felt like he'd fallen from a plane. With no parachute.

~~~~

In Matt's apartment, Zachery was tuning Dev's vintage radio and heard Sinatra's smooth voice sing, "*I've got you...under my skin...*" He smiled, remembered seeing young Sinatra through Costanza's eyes in 1938 at the Astor Roof, singing with Tommy Dorsey's band. And afterward getting hammered with Frank and Lucky Luciano.

As Zachery opened the fridge and took a slug from a bottle of pear juice he'd bought, his cell beeped. He answered, "This is Shaw."

"Mr. Shaw, my name is Letitia Lewis at JPMorgan Chase. I'm sorry for any inconvenience today. But our system is now back online and all accounts in your portfolio are in order."

"Excellent. And about goddamn time!" He clicked off, smiling triumphantly as he heard a key unlocking the door.

Molly entered, shaking off her wet hair and clothes. "It's freezing rain out there. I am completely—" His pleasantly satiated expression stopped her. "You look like the cat who ate a *flock* of canaries."

"But I'm still famished." Zachery stood and abruptly pulled her close, startling her with a surprisingly intense—and very deep— kiss. Then nuzzled her neck, purring, "Let's go to Venice."

"Mmm, I could be persuaded," she murmured, "after midterms."

"Wonderful." He was unbuttoning her blouse. "Meanwhile, I'll give you a preview."

Moments later, they were down to their underwear, rolling onto the bedroom futon. His intensity increased. She was curious, but also stimulated. He spoke, lips-to-lips, between his aggressive kisses. "You feel...wonderful..."

She came up for air. "Well, thanks, but what's—" he momentarily stopped her mouth with another kiss "—what's up with you? You'd think that we hadn't done it in a month!"

"Feels much longer, my dear."

"*'My dear'?*"

"Yes! It's an entirely new me." He dived in again, more intensely, clawing at her breasts, pulling at her bra.

"Wait, wait!" She slipped it off as he discarded his jockey shorts, then ran his hands like paint brushes down across her breasts and on down her sides, snagging her panties on the way, pulling them off roughly. "Hey! Slow down, Matt! I'm not going anywhere."

His face came back up to hers. He tried to pace himself as he buried his face in her hair, inhaled her fragrance, his eagerness escalating. Between kisses he said, "Did your friend...like that Mencken book?"

"Thinks he's—" she succumbed momentarily to his probing tongue "—kind of harsh."

"Ah," Zachery said, "I'm quite fond of old HL." His fingertips pressed into her thighs. "I love what he said about the American people..." He rolled fully on top of her. *The most timorous, sniveling, poltroonish, ignominious mob...*" He kissed her firmly, then worked his open mouth down her neck. *"...of serfs and goose-steppers ever gathered under one flag since the end of the Medieval Ages."*

Molly was unsure what was going on but getting caught up in his ardor. "I didn't know you...knew so much about him."

"There's a whole world in me you have yet to discover."

He flipped her over roughly, pulled her aggressively onto her hands and knees. She was startled. "Hey! What's gotten into you?!"

"Aren't you more interested in what's getting into *you?*" He thrust hard.

"Ow!" she gasped, "Wait! *Ow!* ... Matt? ... *Wait!*"

Zachery ignored her, thrusting again and again, harder. But Molly suddenly dropped forward. Moving like a panther, twisting over to face him, she pulled her knees up under his crotch to lift his hips as she stiff-armed his shoulders up decisively. "What part of '*Wait*' don't you understand?!"

He was surprised by her agility and defensive skill. "Stronger than you look."

"And trained to fight off jerks, don't forget."

Stimulated by the competition, still hovering over her, his blue eyes flashed.

But hers were commanding. She shoved him aside. "Stay! Right. There."

She rolled up onto her knees, saying, "Call me paranoid, but if

Zachery was having us watched before, I don't want it to happen again."

Zachery eyed her lithe form she reached for the window's curtains.

Matt had taken the express subway downtown, then rushed through the falling sleet on his shaky, straining legs toward his flat. He was hoping to intercept Molly, to convince her of the truth before she fell completely into Zachery's hands. As he arrived on the icy sidewalk across Bank Street, he looked up and saw Molly's smiling face and bare shoulders inside the flat's window. He saw her grasp its curtain, saw Zachery's hand reach up to stroke her arm. Matt waved desperately with both hands, hoarsely shouting, "Molly! No!" She didn't hear and pulled the curtains closed; unaware he was below.

Matt's heart twisted painfully. Tears welled in his bloodshot eyes. He was trembling, nauseous, choking back bile, knowing what Zachery was doing up there with an unsuspecting Molly. But Matt also knew any intervention he might attempt would only get him arrested, permanently locked away, and merely postpone Zachery's pleasuring himself with her.

Matt slumped against a barren tree, his breaths showing in the frigid air. He was devastated from witnessing the torturous travesty. His entire body ached with the deep, impossible yearning for it to be yesterday. He was yearning for his life, his Village, his friends, his hopes and dreams of successful cancer research. And Molly. All lost, and worse: he was wanted by the police, incriminated in murders and—Matt half-laughed at the calamitous, surreal complexity of his situation. Then he suddenly felt faint, chilled and shivering from the freezing rain. He coughed painfully into his hand. On his wrinkled palm Matt saw droplets of blood.

Perfect, he thought sardonically. The perfect end to a perfect day.

He started to move off. Stopped. Looked around helplessly. A cold fog was settling in making the dark street that had been his neighborhood seem more forbidding, soulless, like nothing he recognized, with every door closed.

He had no idea what to do, where to go.

Chapter 13

The sleet and fog had evolved into a misting icy drizzle that was even colder, more bitter. The frail old gentleman had wandered through the dreary gloom aimlessly, painfully onto Seventh Avenue South. His mind was working, but no solutions presenting. Instead, constantly unfolding in his brain were images of his bedroom, his futon, the love of his life nude and believing she was having intercourse with him while actually being intertwined with an unworthy, patently evil imposter. Worse still, Matt knew how the triumphant, arrogant Zachery was relishing every aspect of her fragrance, the feel of her skin, the tastes of Molly as he ravished her and she welcomed it all lovingly, happily, unknowingly.

With a sudden roar of hatred, Matt pulled off his glasses and fiercely rubbed his eyes trying to staunch the unbidden imageries. He looked around for some place, any place, he might escape his imaginings. In the misty distance he saw an all-night cybercafé.

Its interior was rattier than the one where he'd had his last hopeful call with Thelma. He felt bitter sadness for her death and agonizing responsibility for causing it. He sat disconsolately at a computer. Finally, though knowing it was a waste of time, he listlessly logged into his Med-X email.

His main menu came up. It took a moment for his tired eyes to realize he had a video message. He instantly became alert. He inhaled, clicked the video icon. An image appeared of Thelma from her monitor's camera.

"Hey, boyo," she said cheerily. "You're probably on your way back, but I didn't want to wait. I think I found it!"

Matt's heart rate increased. He shifted with agitation on the wooden chair, leaned closer to the screen. He heard the sound of Thelma's door buzzer. She glanced back over her shoulder, calling out, "Skeeter? I'm right in the middle of—"

"Yeah, I got it, Thel." Skeeter headed across the drawing room.

Thelma looked right into her camera—right into Matt's tense eyes. "I found it in an ancient manuscript related to *The Book of Kells.*"

As Skeeter walked toward the front door his head tilted up slightly, as though sensing something pleasant. "It's just 'them' again."

"Who?" Thelma said. "I'll be there in a sec."

"Oh, no," Matt murmured fearfully as he watched Skeeter open the front door. Matt knew Skeeter couldn't see that it was the *other* 'them.' Matt recognized the flimsy jacket, his own jeans. Knew it was 'himself.' But seeing the ski mask and gloves, Matt drew a frightened breath.

Thelma was unaware of the threat, spoke enthusiastically to Matt, "That final word we're looking for seems to be something like—"

"Hang on!" Skeeter cried out, trying to block the door. "You ain't right!"

Thelma heard his cry, turned to look. "Skeeter? What's wrong?!"

Matt clenched. "No! Thelma!"

Skeeter was distressed, yelling, "Thelma! Watch out!"

Thelma leapt from her chair, saw the intruder bludgeon defenseless Skeeter to the floor, club him again, then come toward her. Thelma slammed her study door in his face. Matt heard him pounding it hard.

Thelma rushed frantically back toward her computer, fearing for her life but determined. She said forcefully, "It's *'Rek-wee!'* Matt! It's *'Rek-wee!'*"

The door behind her exploded inward, Thelma spun to defend herself against the young man wearing a ski mask who attacked her brutally, shoving her right toward the camera. Her hand aimed for her keyboard.

The video window went black.

Matt sat unmoving. Unable to breathe.

~~~~

THE SHOT GLASS ON THE CYBERCAFÉ BAR WAS BEING FILLED with whiskey for the second time. Matt's trembling, age-spotted hand lifted it as his other hand put a pain pill in his mouth. He swallowed it with the fiery liquid. He coughed, covering his mouth with a cocktail napkin, and saw several drops of blood on it. He was staggered by the nightmare tragedy on Thelma's email. Then he carefully took out the talisman. He turned it in his fingers, speaking low, measuring the words.

"...*Awat ah-lone sin yah, tahm walla tey...rek-wee.*"

He stared at the talisman. Thinking at what dreadful cost he'd learned the powerful phrase.

"Say what?"

Matt glanced down the bar at a late-twenties man. He wore jeans and a blue-collar shirt with a logo for Edgerton Construction and nodded a greeting. "Just wonderin' what you said. Some kinda toast?"

Matt shook his head. "No."

"Too bad, I always like learnin' new ones." He lifted his beer mug. "Y'know, like 'skol,' 'l'chaim.' Here's a Persian one: 'Beh sala-maty!' Just means 'to your health,' but it impresses chicks." He winked. "So, what did that mean, what you said?"

Matt's aged thumb and forefinger rubbed the talisman. "It's a curse."

"Damn! That's even better!" He slid one stool closer. "Tell me about it."

Matt felt completely done in, his old voice so quiet the guy could barely hear. "You don't want to know."

The young guy eyed the talisman and couldn't resist asking, "What's that? Some kinda medal?"

"No." Matt shook his head without looking. "It's...very old. It's..."

"Can I?" He reached out his hand.

Matt glanced at him, hesitated, then placed the talisman in the palm of the man's muscular hand.

"Boy, that sombitch really *feels* old, don't it? And a guy with two faces, huh?"

Matt was carefully scrutinizing the young construction worker. In the prime of life. Unsuspicious.

A muffling, foreboding strangeness suddenly encompassed Matt. The room and the world outside the café window had fallen into slow-motion. Sounds echoed distantly, including the young guy's voice, which rolled out low-pitched and slowed down to one syllable at a time.

"So...what...is...it...? What's...this...thing...for?"

Matt's breathing grew shallow. He looked at the talisman in the young man's palm. Then saw a shaker of salt, a nearby glass of water.

He realized it would be...so very easy.

The guy's face floated slowly closer, prompting, "Come...on... man..."

Matt looked into the bright, encouraging, naive eyes for an extended moment.

Then Matt clenched his teeth. Forced himself to inhale. *Sharply.*

That burst the dreamy bubble of isolation. Broke the spell, like startling awake. The café was back to normal as the determined young guy eagerly prodded, "You gotta tell me, man!"

But a new thought had occurred to Matt. He retrieved the dangerous talisman, glanced apologetically at the man. "I can't. I'm sorry."

Then he hurried out into the night.

~~~~

In the Med-X lab, only four or five others were embroiled in their work on the graveyard shift across the room, so Dev hadn't put on a hair cover. His computer station was in one of only two quadrants which were fully illuminated at night. He was organizing a recent data dump as he answered his landline phone. "Bhandari, Lab One."

"Hey," a voice whispered, "It's Matt. Come out to the back alley. It's important."

Having put on his North Face jacket, Dev used his security card to unlock the back door. He carefully opened it a fraction to peer out. The rain had stopped but everything was wet. Dev was dumbfounded to see Dr. John Zachery wearing a knit cap and trench coat, sitting disconsolately on a shipping box, coughing, nearly spent.

~~~~

AN HOUR LATER, ALMOST 2AM, HAVING HEARD EVERYTHING, Dev stood thunderstruck. He was fearfully double-checking something on his phone while glancing down at the old professor emeritus whose breath showed in the frigid air. Finally, Dev shook his head emphatically. "No...not possible." He waved the cell phone. "If Thelma Greer had been killed it would be hyper-viral by now and there is *nothing!*"

"I *told* you, I asked the cops not to release any info." Matt was irritated. "And while the phone's in your hand, will you empty your goddamn voice mailbox!"

"But it's all crazy. Impossible!" Dev stared, shaken but certain. "I don't believe you."

"For God's sake, Dev!" Matt's basso voice bellowed, "you believe that *l-lizard people* are running the UN!"

"That's totally different. Makes more sense, because—" A sudden quirky smile twisted onto Dev's face. "Waaaait a minute." Dev suddenly felt like a fool. Couldn't believe he'd been so gullible. "Matt put you up to this, didn't he? That son of a bitch. How did he actually talk someone like you into—"

Matt jumped up, grabbed Dev's jacket collar hard. "Goddammit, it's the *truth!* It's n-not somewhere *'out there!'* It's right *here* in your face!"

"Whoa! Take it easy, Dr. Zach—!"

"I can't take it easy!" Matt shouted as he shook Dev fiercely. "This body I'm in is *dying!*" He was trembling, urgent. "Quiz me, Dev! Okay? I'm M-Matt!" He released his grasp, took a half-step back. "Just ask! Ask me anything!"

"My mother's name?"

"Lakshmi!"

Dev shook his head, "Way too easy. Anybody could've—"

"No. Please, Dev— Okay. Then s-something more obscure."

"Obscure?"

"Yes! Something that went down just between us."

Dev pondered a moment. "Okay. Okay: last night. When you came in from dinner."

"Yes? What? Wh-what?"

"I was looking at something on the web?"

"It was," Matt struggled to remember, "It was…was…A UFO!"

"You could've guessed that."

"No. That was it!"

"Then where was the sighting?"

"Oh, come on," Matt was distraught, flailing. "I was drunk! I don't—"

"Riiiight," Dev was sarcastic, heading for the back door. "I'm sorry, sir. This was interesting for a while. You really helped Matt play a funny joke. Really had me going, but let's give it a rest." He used his security card to unlock the door.

Matt was desperate. "No, Dev! Please. Wait! I can show you a video that—"

Dev guffawed, "AI can fake *anything*." He pulled the door open. "Tell Matt ha-ha for me."

Dev walked inside. The door was closing. Then Matt had a flash, shouted, *"Kanab! It was in Kanab. Utah!"*

But the door clicked closed. Locked.

Matt sagged. Heartbroken.

Then the door clicked again. Very slowly, Dev peered back out. Wide-eyed. Ashen.

~~~~

AT DEV'S STATION IN THE MED-X LAB THEY WERE WATCHING Thelma's video email. Dev held his breath, his hand clutching his own throat as he watched the ski-masked "Matt" bludgeon Skeeter and attack Thelma. When the screen went black, Dev sat aghast, having witnessed the brutal murder of two human beings, one of whom Dev idolized.

Tears welled in his eyes. He could barely whisper, "It is... beyond...anything."

He looked at the old man sitting beside him, now wearing a white lab coat over his clothes. Matt's wrinkled gray-green eyes also shined with tears.

Dev squeezed the old man's arm—the arm of his closest friend imprisoned inside the dying body. Matt was equally agonized over the loss of Skeeter and Thelma Greer. His throat was choked with emotion. "And it's because of me, Dev. It's m-my fault."

"No way, Matt!"

"Yes. If I hadn't gone to them—"

"You had no way of knowing he'd go there. And why would Zachery even think you *had* gone to—" Dev's face suddenly went white, looking shocked to his core. "Oh, Great God!" Dev's hands went to his head as he gasped, "It was *me!*"

"What?" Matt was confused. "No. That's not even—"

"Yes, yes!" Matt was startled as Dev dug his fingers deep into his tall pile of hair, clenching fistfuls of it in frantic distress. "I was getting on a bus for the con when I saw you—*him*—and I shouted to him—" Dev struggled to keep his voice a whisper so others working across the room wouldn't hear. He was fighting hysteria with tears in his eyes. "—I shouted that I hadn't heard back from

Thelma. That's why he went there!" Dev put his face down on his desk, still clutching his hair, white-knuckled, quaking with silent sobs.

Matt leaned closer, rested his age-spotted hand on Dev's back.

Several profound minutes passed in silence as they each internalized the responsibility they felt. At length, Dev raised back up and they stared at each other, a monumental weight of guilt crushing them. Then Dev glanced at the black screen. He sniffed his runny nose, wiped his eyes and wet cheeks, finally said softly, "Well, I can tell you one thing for sure, Mattsy." A faint, wistful smile crossed Dev's face. "And you saw it for yourself in that video. Dr. Thelma Greer died while doing exactly what she loved: fighting to help someone."

The old man met his friend's gaze, nodded agreement.

Dev squared his shoulders, took a deep breath. "Show it to me."

Matt lifted the talisman from his pocket.

Dev eyed it. So small. So insignificant. "And all you have to say is…"

"That phrase. Y-yeah. And *boom*." Matt's arthritic fingers held it out. "Want a taste?"

"Decidedly not." Then Dev drew a resolute breath. "But I will tell you what I *do* want."

There was a never-before-seen deadly fire in Dev's eyes. Matt understood, saying, "Retribution. For Thelma."

"Yes…" Dev's throat was tight. He could barely speak. "…and for Skeeter."

They gazed at each other, agreed. But they knew the odds against them were massive.

And that their path ahead was decidedly unclear.

Chapter 14

A few hours later, it was late morning in the Bleeker Street flat. Dev walked out of his room, yawning, his eyes dark from too little sleep. His roommate was shirtless at the table having his juice, a bagel, and a Tums. He seemed to be pleasantly engaged, greatly enjoying the financial reports on his cell.

Dev's mind was replaying Matt's astonishing story as he tried to act everyday-normal, getting a bagel, while surreptitiously glancing at his college pal. He casually asked, "How's it going, man?"

"Very satisfactorily."

"Well, I hope that doesn't mean more cigars around here."

Zachery smirked as his cell rang. He answered, "Hello? Yes, this is Matthew."

Zachery heard a woman's voice say, "Matthew, this is Dr. Bleifer over at the University Health Center. We did your insurance physical?"

Zachery pulled his lower lip. "Dr. Bleifer, yes?"

Dev recognized that name, was suddenly alert. He glanced over, curious.

Dr. Bleifer was in her personal office checking a file attachment. "I'm afraid the policy can't go into force yet. One of the tests from your physical came back a little off."

Zachery frowned, "What do you mean 'off'?"

"You remember we diagnosed you having SIBO? That's small intestine—"

"Small Intestine Bacterial Overgrowth, yes," Zachery said impatiently, "and I also clearly remember being told that SIBO was nothing to be concerned about."

"And that's true, but the insurance company requested a second look at data and caught an anomaly, which means—"

"I know goddamn well what an anomaly is. I'm not a moron." Zachery was pacing now.

Dev also knew an anomaly meant something was not normal. He kept a discreet distance, but was getting concerned as he heard Zachery say, "But you said he passed—that *I* passed—all the tests. You told me I was in good health. Nothing wrong."

"And nothing may be wrong," Bleifer assured her patient. "Another blood sample should clear up any confusion, Matthew. Can you come back over this—"

"I'm coming now!" Zachery snorted, hanging up on the doctor. He pulled on a sweatshirt and snatched his jacket.

Dev watched him carefully, unsettled by what he'd heard. "What is it, man?"

Zachery yanked their front door open, saying gruffly, "Some goddamn dim-wit made a stupid mistake." Then he was gone.

~~~~

AT THE SEVENTH AVENUE CYBERCAFÉ, THE OLD ANGLO-African gentleman had returned. He was using Google Earth to zoom in the satellite image of Manhattan toward the Guggenheim Museum on Fifth Avenue.

The eye-in-the-sky view showed three small, narrow buildings on Eighty-eighth Street just east of the museum. Matt switched to street-level view. One townhouse was just as Dean Sanger had described: right up against the back of the Guggenheim. He saw it was a beautiful 1910-era neoclassical, stone and brick building. Its second-floor balcony over the entrance portico was supported by two Doric Greek columns. Matt zoomed in the camera toward the wrought-iron double doors on the front. He could read the street number in leaded glass above them. It was 5 EAST 88TH.

He stared at it for a moment, then his arthritic fingers fumbled to unzip the shirt pocket where he'd put the key ring taken from Zachery's mansion. He flipped through the keys again. No numbers, but one had what he thought was a tiny letter S.

He squinted closer through his wireframes but couldn't be sure. He held the key out to a young woman at the next computer. "S-sorry to interrupt, but my old eyes can't tell. What does this look like to you?"

She peered at it. "Like a 5."

~~~~

IN THE NYU MEDICAL EXAM ROOM, A FEMALE TECH GLANCED at Matthew Shaw's admirable six-pack as she did a slow blood pull. Zachery was shirtless after a brief physical exam and greatly resented being there. He swallowed uneasily, his stomach apparently queasy.

Dr. Bleifer typed her notes into the room's computer station. "I also want to do a small biopsy."

"For what?" Zachery groused.

"It's probably nothing, Matthew, but with your family history—"

"What are you talking about?" Zachery's annoyance was increasing. "I have every right to—"

"Of course," the doctor said quietly. She waited for the nurse to exit with the samples, closing the door. "We know that your mother died from stomach cancer."

Zachery's young blood chilled. "What are you saying?"

"I just want to rule it out, that's all."

~~~~

MATT WAS BREATHING HEAVILY, HURRYING ALONG ICY EAST Eighty-Eighth Street toward Central Park, Fifth Avenue, and the spiraling Guggenheim. He eyed the five-story townhouse he'd seen online nestled up against the museum. He looked up at the beautiful bay windows on the second through the fifth floor. The tall colonnaded entrance portico had a balustrade along its top with a statuary cherub mounted at each end. They were smiling down at him. On either side of the entrance Matt noted window boxes with some evergreens surviving the November weather. He climbed up the wide stone steps to the wrought-iron double door. There was a large beveled-glass window in the door, but a curtain attached within prevented seeing inside. Matt's age-spotted hand trembled slightly as he tried to insert the proposed key. With a slight jostling, it fit in. He turned it successfully.

Matt slipped inside, closing and locking the door. His wheezing voice called out, "Hello? Anyone here?" No answer. He stood in the small marble foyer; just beyond it was a high-ceilinged room, elegantly appointed with late nineteenth and early twentieth century furniture, statuary, classical oil paintings and such. Matt recalled being in a similar place only once before.

When he was eighteen, a donor to the National Geographic Society held a reception at a Park Avenue mansion to celebrate Matt's mother and her archeological team for discovering the frozen Andes man. Matt remembered how brave his mother had been that night, cheerfully greeting the attendees while completely hiding her pain from cancer.

This townhouse of Zachery's was equally baronial. Matt coughed painfully as he walked across the thick carpets amid the furnishings. Some were draped with gossamer-thin sheets to avoid dust. They lent an uneasy, ghostly ambience. Reaching the base of an opulent staircase, he looked up. "Anyone up there?" he shouted, which made him cough. No answer came. Matt drew a breath and made his frail body slowly climb the oak steps.

~~~~

IN THE BLEEKER FLAT, DEV WAS AT HIS WORKTABLE DOING homework online, when the front door banged open. "Whoa! What in—what's wrong?"

His roommate hurtled toward the bathroom, barely making it to the toilet where he dropped to his knees, dry heaving.

Dev came up behind him, nervous and seriously worried. "What's wrong? Matt?"

Zachery sputtered angrily, "Nothing!" Then he vomited voluminously.

Dev grabbed a towel. "No, no, this doesn't look like—"

"It's *nothing*, I'm telling you!" Zachery shouted, between heaves. "It's all bullshit! They took more blood, even did a goddamn biopsy for *no reason!*" He vomited painfully again.

Dev watched, very disturbed, unsure what to do. His heart was pounding.

~~~~

THE FOLLOWING DAY, LATE IN THE AFTERNOON, DR. BLEIFER'S patient Matthew Shaw was ushered into her empty office by a receptionist. "She'll be right with you."

Zachery sat in the leather chair, trying to ignore that he was feeling slightly light-headed. Finally, Dr. Bleifer entered. Her expression was unreadable as she sat behind her desk.

"So?" Zachery asserted arrogantly, "Everything's okay, right?"

"I wish I could say yes, Matthew. But I'm afraid I can't." She sighed. "The new lab reports on your blood work *and* the biopsy indicate stomach cancer."

The air around Zachery dropped below freezing.

He sat motionless.

Then he laughed, assuredly. "Well." He shook his head. "*That* can't be right."

Dr. Bleifer's profound expression said the opposite.

Zachery sniffed with supreme confidence, demanding, "I want a second opinion."

"Of course." She pushed two files across her desk toward him, saying quietly, "I already got two others. Dr. Elkins you know from your exam here and Dr. Madison is my colleague at Sinai. As soon as they saw yesterday's blood work and biopsy results, they concurred." She paused, then reluctantly added, "And it's Stage Four."

Zachery scanned one file meticulously. Then the second. He dropped them back on the desk as he stood and paced slowly in the small office, astonished by the outrageous irony. Unwilling to accept it. His agile mind was working swiftly, taking charge. "Contact the Mayo Clinic and—what's that other—City of Hope? And understand, money is no problem, so—"

"Dr. Elkins used to teach at both. Before giving me his opinion, he confidentially sent your information to his colleagues at Mayo and at Hope. You'll see that at the bottom of his file. They all concurred. Unfortunately, Matthew, money is not the issue. Your body is."

Zachery glanced sharply at her, pausing as the gravity took hold. Then he snapped, "So, how long?"

"Well," she drew a breath, "carcinoma of the stomach is one of the most aggressive—"

"How long?" Zachery was petulant.

"A month—maybe." Dr. Bleifer shook her head. "I'm truly sorry, Matthew... I've made preliminary arrangements for immediate hospice so you can have the most comfortable—"

"Fuck that." Zachery spat. He jerked her door open, shouting venomously, *"Fuck you all!"*

The young man stormed out furiously, startling everyone in the office.

Reaching the downstairs lobby, Zachery angrily shoved open the glass door and went into the icy air on the health center's terrace. He was fuming, calculating the situation. His eyes flitted this way and that—catching momentarily on a dark-skinned student with a pile of black hair rounding a corner. Bhandari? It didn't matter to Zachery or to the broiling neurons in his distressed brain that were scrambling to sort life-or-death possibilities.

As he walked the Village streets Zachery's agitated mind kept plumbing all the damnable aspects of his circumstances. His belly was increasingly troubled, knotting up. Gray clouds overhead grew denser, hastening the evening twilight.

Zachery was almost to Bleeker and Bank when he felt acid rising in his chest. Three pedestrians who recognized him in the neighborhood were startled as the normally friendly young man rudely shoved them out of his way, rushing into his building.

He dashed into the flat's kitchen, painfully heaving bile into the sink. It was a small amount, but concentrated. He downed a cup of water, but his throat still burned. From the fridge he gulped down the remainder of his pear juice, but even it didn't relieve the sourness.

Or his turbulent emotions.

He leaned both fists heavily on the kitchen table, glancing around like an angry tiger. It was too absurd. To imagine that this was where his magnificent, unprecedented existence might end was positively preposterous. Face down on the filthy floor in a ratty flat with shabby, trash-heap furnishings? He regarded his surroundings with disgust and detestation. Would this roach-infested shithole witness his termination, become his crypt? After all the extraordinary grandeur he'd enjoyed: the royal castles, the doge palaces, oligarchic mansions, intercontinental aircraft, sultanic yachts he'd frequented? Including many he owned personally?

His brain percolated up flashes of days and nights across the centuries: his mobster cronies kowtowing, opening satchels of Prohibition cash; the 1840s slaver captain displaying a chest of gold coins. Memories cascaded through his addled brain: of Marie Antoinette eyeing him intimately in her Louvre Palace boudoir; of the smirking, brilliantly shrewd Catherine de Medici, whose ruthlessness he co-opted; the saucy glances from Elizabeth the First at Hampton Court in 1602; the fireworks exploding in the dark sky, showering their flurries of sparks over her Royal Flotilla, the sparkles reflected on the surface of the nighttime Thames as he watched among Elizabeth's other favorites on her Royal Barge.

He recalled the power he'd savored when condemning the women in Salem who'd spurned him. And the carnal exuberances he'd felt living his unbridled life, feeding his insatiable sexual appetites, having his rapacious way with so many desirable women.

He remembered how each looked at him with ecstasy—or terror—in their eyes as he pleasured himself with them, often brutally. Some were willing, eager, but many—including Matthew's angry mother—fought back, which only urged him to escalate his aggression.

There came flashes also of academic audiences applauding him, plus politicians, industrialists, military commanders and royals who'd prized his counsel. So many were continually astounded by his depth of wisdom derived from his incomparable, insightful, seemingly first-hand knowledge of history. He'd delighted in their adulation of him in grandiose, opulent chambers from the present century back through the fourteenth, thirteenth, twelfth centuries and earlier. Their voices echoed in his brain praising him obsequiously for his financial successes and political triumphs that enriched them – and himself most of all. He relished the power he'd wielded over everyone and everything. Including Death.

Until now.

He'd successfully inhabited yet another youthful body—only to discover it was cancer-ridden, dying. He laughed aloud bitterly at the outrageous irony.

Zachery found himself staring down at the threadbare Persian rug he'd wandered onto in the center of the despicably ugly, contemptible flat. Looking up, he caught his reflection in the mirror gazing back from its dented frame on the cracked wall. He stepped closer, studying his current young face.

As he stared, the image blurred, morphing into fleeting glimpses of his previous reflections: John Zachery, then Alberto Costanza, then slave-trader McClain, then face after different face flickering by like pages in a flipbook. An accelerating backwards spectrum of his former faces: broad, narrow, brawny, effete, long-haired, short-haired, balding, clean-shaven or with beards or moustaches from bushy, mutton-chopped, formal, handlebar. With skin tones Nordic-white to Mediterranean to rustic-ruddy to Moorish.

In varied headgear: fedoras, top hats, knit caps, powdered wigs or Sun-King-foppish adornments.

Until the images came to a stop on his *Original Face*.

A medieval young man. Early twenties, underweight, with stringy, shoulder-length hair. A makeshift bandage covered his right eye. Above and below the patched eye were recent, unhealed, ghastly claw wounds. But the left eye stared back at Zachery from within the mirror.

Zachery could see that behind the young man in the mirror was a torch-lit, smoky, 450AD castle chamber that he well-remembered standing in that day. Several knights, two wearing chain mail, sat or stood, all drinking, laughing, around a very large, rustic, round table. They paused respectfully as their newlywed monarch entered. They bowed to honor their young king.

Then Zachery saw a beautiful, beguiling young maiden edge up closely behind the bandaged young man's shoulder. Her two blue eyes met the youth's single eye in the mirror. She placed her hand delicately atop his shoulder as she smiled privately, remembering—as Zachery also did—the highly-agreeable, dangerously-clandestine intimacy they shared. The young man nodded rakishly to the lovely maiden, murmuring, "M'lady Guinevere…" Then he blinked, realized his error, and smirked, correcting himself. "Forgive me…" He inclined his head slightly, with mock respect, whispering, "Your… *Majesty.*"

Their sensual gaze held as Zachery looked closer into the mirror and saw the thin gold chain around the medieval young man's neck, then a glimpse inside his shirt of his chest and the talisman.

Zachery instinctively clutched at his own chest where the talisman should have been.

But wasn't.

Volcanic rage suddenly surged up in Zachery and erupted with an ear-splitting roar. He grabbed a wooden chair, swung it hard, and fractured the mirror. He smashed it again, knocking it off the wall. In wild-eyed fury, he bashed a lamp aside, then swung the chair down like a sledgehammer on the makeshift bricks-and-boards bookshelf, disintegrating it to rubble. Puffing like a bull from the exertion, he stumbled, landed on hands and knees, staring at the floor. On it, he saw multiple reflections of his infuriated young face in fragmented pieces of the mirror. All glaring up at him.

Zachery's stomach cramped into an excruciating knot, a piercing reminder of his reality. Yet he refused to accept defeat. He pulled himself up onto a chair, undaunted. *No!* he shouted inwardly. *There must be a solution! I have wealth beyond imagining! I'll buy a new jet tonight! I'll buy a fleet of them! Assemble a team to search—to scatter and search— wherever! There must be other goddamned doctors! Or off-the-radar alternatives, other experts who could—! I can pay whatever the hell is necessary to—!*

"Money is not the issue." The doctor's words cut sharply through his frantic ramblings. Her words—and worse—her clinical evidence, laid siege to his fevered brain:

"Money is not the issue." Her voice echoed with finality, "*Your body is.*"

That hobbled him. His head collapsed onto his chest. He sat there seething, panting. Without the talisman, he was trapped. He'd never before been in this disastrous position. Always, in years past, he'd easily retrieved it by bribery, subterfuge, or murder.

He sat, seeming to feel his enemy within eating away, destroying him cell by cell even as his mind wandered on, trying to formulate a way to save himself, trying to get a glimpse into his future. But his efforts proved circuitous, always returning to the dark reality of his impending doom. For the first time in fifteen hundred years, he saw only emptiness.

Darkness slowly settled outside. Shadows deepened in the room. Finally, the only faint light slanted in from a single street-lamp down the street below.

At length, Zachery noticed within the gloom a tiny pin-point of light blinking. During his rampage, Dev's vintage answering machine had apparently picked up a call. Zachery ignored it. He sat limply. Unmoving.

But after a long moment, he looked again. It blinked.

He went to it, angrily stabbed the play button, then reacted sharply when he heard his own deep voice. It was very weak but fuming. "I can't believe it! Goddammit, Dev, your fucking c-cell mailbox…is still full!—*Shit!*" The voice sounded near crying with misery, struggling to breathe. Zachery was keenly attentive. "Alright, Dev…listen, I n-need to see you…pretty quick…'cause I'm… r-really slipping, pal. My alveoli must have started rupturing… I'm coughing blood and—" he was short of breath— "I'm on the fourth floor…of that townhouse I told you about…by the G-Guggenheim."

Zachery blinked, astounded.

"The k-key's in a window box…by the porch. But come alone…I don't w-want Molly to…see me die like this… Just hurry, Dev…I've got to talk to you before—"

The machine clicked off. Zachery stared at it.

Chapter 15

An hour later, in the opulent fourth-floor master bedroom of 5 East Eighty-Eighth Street, the body of Dr. John Zachery was lying fully clothed atop a midnight-blue, silk bedspread on an antique English four-poster. A small, portable respirator was feeding oxygen through thin tubes to his nose. He was gazing to one side at his reflection in a wall mirror. His elderly body appeared very weak. His face had a sodden, sickly look. The multitudinous wrinkles at the corners of his eyes had deepened.

The only light in the room came from a Waterford cut-crystal lamp beside the bed, and another with a sculpted bronze dancer as a base on a table by a chair at the end of the bed. Hearing a slight noise, Matt was shocked to see "himself" entering.

Matt felt his old heart flutter. "How'd *you* f-find me?" He tried not to let his anxiety show. "How'd you get in?"

Zachery closed the door. From across the room, Matt saw Zachery's young face was taut, that he looked unusually pale. Zachery spoke matter-of-factly, "I have some magical methods."

Matt inhaled, hurting. "Merlin always did."

Zachery's eyebrows raised, surprised. "Very good! And quite close. But no cigar."

"Then who are you?"

His paranormal nemesis meandered restlessly toward a side

desk, unable to conceal hints of physical discomfort. "Ever hear the orchestral piece by Paul Dukas? *The Sorcerer's Apprentice?*" He glanced at Matt. "Sort of became my theme song."

Matt was working to breathe. "So, you were *with* Merlin? And what, you killed him?"

"It was self-defense," Zachery said as he sat against the edge of the desk. "He caught me examining his little masterpiece."

"The talisman."

"He wasn't pleased. Clawed my eye out." Zachery shrugged it off. "He'd have died soon, anyway. I just helped him pass a bit sooner."

"Probably 'helped' Costanza, too… I don't believe it was 'a mob hit.'"

"You'd be correct," Zachery said, seeming distracted by internal uneasiness. "I prefer dispatching my forbearers as soon as it's convenient. Besides, Death takes everyone eventually. Except me." He took a breath. "So. Where's my little Life Achievement award?"

"Hidden away. Where you can't—"

"No, no," Zachery said knowingly, from experience, "I told you: nobody lets it out of reach—particularly when they're dying. Because it's their only way out. People cling to it like a life preserver till their last breath."

"Well, asshole, I'm close…to that," Matt's rasping voice rumbled, "But you'll never find it, so go fuck yourself."

"Oh Matthew," Zachery chided wistfully, "I know you're just playing for time here—expecting Bhandari to arrive and somehow incapacitate me—so you can get your body back. I'm sorry, but he won't be joining us."

Matt tried not to react as Zachery shifted from some abdominal pain and said, "I heard your frantic phone message to him—which was so perfectly timed when *I* was present to 'accidentally' hear it. I realized your sophomoric attempt to lure me here by dangling just enough tantalizing information."

Matt's expression remained steely as Zachery continued, "You did sound desperate—like you might even use the relic *against* *Bhandari*; might trade that rapidly decaying husk of yours for his young flesh." With a faraway glance Zachery recalled, "I've known that desperation. More than once it's driven me to that extreme—exchanging my failing body for a closest friend." He sighed casually, summing it up: *"C'est la vie!"*

Then he raised his index finger toward Matt. "But...I asked myself: would the supremely noble Matthew Shaw be capable of doing that to *his* friend? Or was your desperate-sounding call just a touch of melodrama to add urgency for me to reach you first?"

Matt's face revealed nothing.

"Probably melodrama." Zachery winked. "Which I confirmed by looking down from our window, glimpsing his hideous yellow coat in an alcove on Bank Street. I saw Bhandari watching for me to exit our downstairs door. So, I obliged him. I hurried quickly out the front and into our back alley. When he came around the corner in pursuit, his head encountered a brick—which I'd brought from your bookshelf."

Then he added, with annoyance, "But my blow was *cushioned* by his preposterous pile of hair. And before I could deliver the *coup de grace* a woman appeared with an annoying yapper dog, so I had to depart hastily. I hated to leave Bhandari breathing and the woman kneeling by him with cell phone in hand." He gestured dismissively. "But even if he survives and accuses me—his room-mate—Bhandari's a known fringe-dweller and his story will sound...considerably unreliable."

Matt appeared stoic; Zachery confident. He stood fully upright, though Matt noted he clenched his teeth from an apparent belly flinch as he went toward the door. "Anticipating some difficulty about reaching a satisfactory arrangement with you, I brought this along." He opened the door and beckoned in Molly.

Matt's wrinkled eyes widened. "No!" he coughed. "Molly! Get away from him!"

Molly was equally startled, glanced angrily at her boyfriend just behind her. "This is the 'surprise' you had for me, Matt? What's going on?"

She looked back compassionately at the frail old man who yelled, "No, Molly! Run!"

But in an eyeblink, Zachery's young left arm shot tightly around her waist as his right arm encircled her chest, his right hand placing the razor tip of a boxcutter precisely against her left carotid artery.

Molly struggled. "Let go! What are you—" She gasped as Zachery made a small cut into her neck. A drop of blood appeared.

"Molly!" Matt strained to raise his feeble body up, the oxygen tubes pulling out.

"No, no," Zachery quietly commanded them both, "Don't. Move. Either of you."

Molly's heart raced, staring into the rheumy eyes of anguished eighty-year-old Matt. Her comprehension of the impossible finally dawning. "Oh my God! What you told me...it's *true!?*"

"Yes, yes," Zachery said impatiently, holding her in his vise grip. "Young Matthew is over there, and dear old Dr. Zachery has got you here." He flinched from abdominal pain. "And I really can't waste time, since this young body is unexpectedly doomed, so we need to—"

"What's he talking about?" Molly stammered.

"I d-don't know!" Matt sounded worried.

Zachery spat bitterly, "You inherited your mother's stomach cancer."

"What?" Matt exclaimed, almost laughing. "No! That's not true. I n-never had—"

"It *is* true. I was sold a bad body. New blood tests—and a

biopsy—just proved this one is *dying*," Zachery grumbled, then added ruefully, "Sort of sad, I enjoyed your mother—"

"You *raped her!*" Matt hissed.

Zachery glanced, surprised. Then sluffed, "It was consensual."

"*I saw your goddamned hand over her mouth!*" Matt yelled, as he pushed himself to the edge of the bed.

"Stop there, *boy.*" Zachery warned, his razor threatening Molly, who was thunderstruck.

"That's why my father came after you, isn't it? And you killed him!"

"Merely defended myself. I—"

"Threw him in front of a car! I saw it!"

"Self-defense," Zachery insisted, dismissive. "But since we're dredging history, it's an open question whether he actually *was* your father."

Matt's craggy face clouded, disbelieving.

But Zachery casually affirmed, "Whenever possible I try to keep these migrations in the family."

"Impossible." Matt shook his head, touched his Anglo-African face. "I look nothing like *this!*"

"Agreed. But you do resemble your mother—have her eyes—and you also look very like your *grandmother*—the lily-white woman who gave birth to half-white baby John Zachery. You definitely inherited that woman's color of hair—and skin." He nodded, emphasizing the truth. "I've tracked you since birth."

Zachery grimaced from stomach pain. "But that's all ancient history. So now to business. I'll take the talisman." His left arm still tight around Molly's waist, his right hand slightly repositioned the razor's edge against Molly's throat, where a second drop of blood was following the first. "I'll count to three, then begin a deeper incision."

Molly was frightened, but also angry. Matt glared.

Zachery was dry, businesslike. "Full disclosure: I'm expert at prolonging a moment of agony. So... One... Two..."

"Alright!" Matt shouted.

Zachery nodded. "I knew I could rely on you, Matthew."

Matt opened his hand, holding the talisman. "Come get it, y-you fucker."

"No. Just throw it here."

Matt swallowed hard, considered other options, but was beaten. He tossed the relic onto the thick Persian carpet between them.

Zachery spoke softly to Molly. "Now, you and I shall retrieve it, my dear. First, we'll take a short step forward." Molly stiffened, resistant. "No, no," he cautioned, maintaining his grip around her waist and his right arm across her chest. "We must proceed cautiously. Wouldn't want your carotid accidentally slashed open." Molly was furious but relented. "That's better." Zachery inhaled her fragrance, whispered in her ear, "And I did enjoy *our* intimacy." His grasp tightened. "Now with me: right foot forward..."

Matt was agonized, his old eyes riveted on Molly and "himself" taking the step together.

"And now the delicate part," Zachery instructed Molly, "just bend down slowly with me, pick it up with your right hand."

Molly locked eyes with Matt. Each saw the other's tightly coiled fury.

As she bent with Zachery, Molly extended her hand toward the talisman. When her fingertips were an inch away, she clenched her teeth—then several things happened with blurring speed: Molly's self-defense training kicked in—her outstretched fingers snapped into a fist, her right elbow rammed backwards like a pile driver into Zachery's groin as she twisted sharply to her right—away from the blade—which he dropped as his body slumped forward in shock from her savage blow.

Simultaneously, Matt lunged from the bed, utilizing a last precious reserve of strength he'd concealed. With fiery determination, Matt snatched up the talisman with his left hand while shouldering his slumping adversary, causing him to fall backward onto the rug. Matt's aged right hand grasped his opponent's left wrist and Matt slapped the relic hard onto Zachery's left palm, clasping his own frail hands atop and beneath to keep the talisman sandwiched inside.

Molly saw that Zachery's younger body had the edge, his right fist striking hard at the old man. She grabbed at Zachery's fist as Matt shouted, "*Awat ah-lone sin—*" but a blow to his face stopped him. Matt felt his grip slipping, called out, "Molly! My hands! Help me!"

She fell across Zachery's right shoulder, partly immobilizing his right arm as her hands clasped tightly atop and beneath Matt's hands holding the relic in place against Zachery's palm as Matt shouted, *"Awat ah-lone sin yah, tahm walla tey rek-wee!"*

All three of their bodies convulsed with the powerful electrical shock.

The old man yelped fearfully and fell back, stunned. Molly gasped. Matt's young body trembled with new ownership. "Oh God! Th-Thank God!" He was elated to hear his own voice, feel his youth regained. He held the talisman tightly. Raised halfway up.

Molly had tears in her eyes, panting. "Matt! Is it *you?* Tell me it's—"

"Y-yes!" Matt said, *"Yes!"*

Molly hugged him tightly for a nanosecond, then pivoted angrily toward the dazed Zachery who was on his feeble hands and knees. She pounded at him feverishly, with both fists. "You *monster* — *Monster!*"

"No! Don't!" Zachery wheezed, falling lower, weakly trying to block her furious blows, his deep bass voice pleading desperately, "Stop it! Stop!"

"Never, you bastard!" Molly yelled. Grabbing the heavy bronze table lamp, she ferociously bludgeoned Zachery's head with it again and again.

His deep voice cried out, "Stop it! I'm— Don't! I'm—"

"Never, NEVER!!" Molly shrieked as she slammed the lamp down with both hands and all her might against his bleeding head. Matt pulled her away as the old man collapsed. Molly dropped the lamp. She landed on the floor against Matt, quaking with blind fury.

He held her tightly. "It's o-okay, Moll. It's okay."

They were trying to catch their breath.

Matt looked at the old man's motionless, bloodied face, saw that the wrinkled eyelids were open just a sliver, showing only the whites—which were yellow with spider-webbed broken blood vessels His mouth gaped open grotesquely, missing the bottom denture and teeth.

Matt felt for Zachery's jugular. Then a second time. And a third. Molly was breathless, suddenly afraid. "Oh my God, I didn't mean to—I was just so mad— Is he—?"

"Can't find a pulse. And I felt death pretty close already when I was…inside."

"Oh, God…" She was still staggered, shaky. "It's all so…so—!"

"I know, Moll. But *you?*" He checked the blood smeared on her neck.

"It's not bad. Just stings." She was focused on the talisman in his hand, swallowing hard. "But how could that thing—" Her eyes flicked sharply onto him. She spoke low, feeling a chill. "Matt? … It really is *you?*"

"Yeah. Y-yeah. It really is." One hand went to his head, feeling his thick hair with huge relief. "It's m-me." He brushed away the lock on his forehead. She smiled, recognizing his characteristic move. As he helped her up, she saw him react to pain in his stomach.

"Wait!" She blurted, scared, *"Stomach cancer?* You have—?"

"I'll explain. But we've got to check on Dev because—"

"Oh no!" Molly had frozen. She was looking apprehensively at the bloodied lamp she'd weaponized against the old man. On it were his blood. And her fingerprints.

Matt stopped dead. "Right...right. And on anything else you touched when you came in with—" he realized, looking at his own fingers "—with '*me.*'" He saw the boxcutter lying nearby. He picked it up, retracted the razor and pocketed it.

Molly was already pulling a pillowcase from the bed. "We've got to wipe everything!" She tossed it to Matt as she grabbed a second, asking urgently. "But the *cancer?!*"

"Dev believed my story," Matt said, using the pillowcase to wipe her fingerprints off the bronze lamp. "We realized all NYU medical tests come through Med-X pathology, so we found and altered one of my test results. S-sent it back to the doctor with an urgent note. They did new blood tests—plus a biopsy—and Dev intercepted *that* data, made it all read cancerous. He'd spiked Zachery's juice with some Indian herbs that'd make him cramp up, feel sick, vomitous—" Matt swallowed some bitter bile, "—and *I* still do—but it was vital for Zachery to *believe* what the doctor told him and be desperate to reclaim the r-relic—"

"To use on some other victim. To save himself." She said while wiping down the desk that Zachery had leaned against.

"Of course." Matt retrieved his throwaway cell phone from the old man's pocket. "When Zachery left the doctor, Dev followed him to our flat, texted me so I could call and 'accidentally' let Zachery know where to find me."

"So he'd come here to retrieve that...*thing*—"

"Yeah. And Dev was bringing hypos of h-heavy sedative to take him down, turn the tables on him." Matt shook his head, embarrassed. "'Best laid plans,' huh? We thought we were so goddamn smart, but that s-sonuvabitch figured out our scam, ambushed Dev and—"

"Oh no, Matt!"

"It sounds like he survived." Matt was wiping down the door frame and knob. "Someone saw Dev and I think called 911. But we've g-gotta be sure."

They moved into the hallway, wiped the outside of the bedroom door. "Good," she said, "Now it's just the banister and the downstairs door."

Matt started to turn, but she caught his sleeve, humiliated. "I'm so sorry *I* didn't believe you." Molly touched his cheek.

"It's okay, Moll. And look…" He gestured toward something over her shoulder. She turned to see an ornate mirror on the hallway wall opposite reflecting the two of them standing there. Matt said quietly, "We got out alive."

Molly's voice was soft, lyrical. "Yes…we survived."

They both gazed at the mirror reflecting their faces. Then Matt flinched with stomach distress. His head tilted down, his eyes pinched closed, so he didn't see that Molly continued gazing at her reflection. She looked more deeply, privately, into her own eyes. Her expression becoming subtly triumphant.

Matt moved to the top of the banister, wiped it, and took one step down to clean the next section. He glanced back at Molly. "We better double wipe it all."

She nodded eagerly. Then she re-wiped the top section and followed down one step behind him on the elegant staircase to clean the next section. Molly smiled at the back of Matt's head, her hazel eyes shining with an enchanted glow of complete success and profound satisfaction.

Matt had reached the fourth step when there came a room-shaking roar.

They both turned to see Zachery's howling, bloodied body in mid-leap onto them.

The three crashed down the stairs together to the halfway landing. Matt's head hit the hardwood, triggering vertigo; he crumpled to one side, disoriented.

The talisman landed on the oak floor between Matt and Molly, who was on her back fighting off Zachery's long fingers clawing their way up her body as his booming bass voice bellowed, "Matt! It's me—Molly! *I'm Molly!*"

"No!" Molly screamed, "He's lying, Matt! Get him off me!" She struggled fiercely against her aged but frenetic assailant.

Matt was dazed, trying to get to his knees, losing balance. Trying again.

The right side of the old man's face and his right eye were covered with blood from his head wounds, but his basso profundo voice shouted, "I am Molly, Matt—*She's Zachery!*"

The old man's left eye spotted the talisman. He grabbed it with his left hand as his right hand caught Molly's left wrist. He pressed the talisman into her left palm clenching both of his gnarled, arthritic hands tightly around her left.

Molly screeched with pain, "No! Stop him, Matt! *Kill him!*" She fought like a banshee, beating fiercely on Zachery's bloody face with her free fist, screaming, "Let go of me!"

The old man weakened, but held on, kept his wrinkled hands clamped tightly around the talisman in Molly's palm, his deep voice yelling, "I'm Molly, Matt! Say those words! *Say them!*"

Matt's eyes flashed to the old man, but Molly cried out in tearful desperation, "No, Matt! Don't listen to him! Look at *me!* You know who I am!" Molly gritted her teeth, focusing all her young strength, about to free her hand.

But the old man's voice thundered, *"Matty! Say those fucking words!"*

Matt instantly clamped his hands atop the old man's with Molly's hand barely held within as he shouted, *"Awat ah-lone sin yah, tahm walla tey rek-wee!"*

All three of their bodies shuddered violently with the electrical jolt. Matt was thrown back by it.

Zachery staggered furiously to his feet—body and soul apparently reunited—bellowing with outrage, "Noooo! *You imbecile!*"

He raised his hands to attack, but together Matt and Molly shoved him with all their combined strength causing Zachery to fall backwards. He crashed through the large beveled-glass window of the landing and fell three stories to hit hard on the cobblestones of the small courtyard below.

Gasping for breath, Molly and Matt looked down from the window. Zachery's ancient body quivered in violent death throes a thousand years overdue.

And suddenly he was still. From beneath his head, blood began to pool.

Molly turned away, trembling with shredded nerves. "Oh my God!" Panicky tears were blinding her. "Oh my God! It was horrible!" Her heart was fibrillating. "I felt so trapped inside him! I felt like—"

"I know *ex-exactly* how you felt." Matt held her tightly, panting hard.

After a moment Molly let herself glance uneasily down toward the courtyard, her quivering hands wiping her eyes and running nose. "What…what are we going to do?"

Matt's mind had been racing, weighing everything. "Probably," he swallowed hard, still trying to think through all the options, "probably best…we just quietly get out of h-here." She shook her head fearfully, but he held her shoulders, steadying her as he added it up. "Think about it, Moll: his staff, his lawyer, they're all convinced he had dementia, making crazy-insane claims, getting aggressive at the library. Then I went to Thelma Greer for help—"

"Dev's Thelma?!"

"Yes. She and her amazing friend found the answers, but they were—" he choked back sudden emotion, reliving the scene "—were…killed by the 'other Matt.'"

Molly went ashen as he confirmed, "It was a nightmare, Molly. A terrible tragedy." He looked inward, tight-lipped, grieving.

She touched his arm, sharing his pain. Then he said, "But when he attacked them he wore gloves, so it's *Zachery's* fingerprints that are all over Thelma's place—police already think he killed them. And Dev knows the truth. If he survived okay, he won't blame *me* for attacking him." Matt glanced at the shattered window. "So, whatever happened here was just…I don't know…maybe a botched r-robbery attempt or—"

Molly glanced sharply at Matt, her spine suddenly an icicle. Her entire body stiffened.

Matt was startled. "What?" She took a step back, her laser eyes boring into him. "Molly?"

"What do you think of HL Mencken?"

"What?" He looked at her blankly. "Who's that?"

She wanted to believe he was telling the truth, but her eyes narrowed. "My essay about Pettus Bridge, Bloody Sunday: what adjectives did you say I should cut?"

"Adjectives? What're you—" Matt looked befuddled. Her focus grew more piercing. "Uh…uh…" he mumbled, squinting, "It was…s-something…and…I think, 'heroically'?"

She exhaled with relief. "You *are* my hero." She hugged him. "But how'd *you* know which was really *me?*"

"Because you told me to say the words. He would've known them. And you'd only heard 'em once."

"Right! God! They were so weird!"

"And you called me Matty."

"Did I?" Her warmth rekindled. "Guess it came naturally." She gently touched his forehead lock. "But what *was* that language? And all that about him and your parents and—"

"Wait." Matt grasped her wrist, focusing hard on her eyes. It was his turn for certainty. "What's the game you play about people in a group?"

"'Game?'"

Matt stared at her intensely. Waiting.

She seemed puzzled, nervous. "'I play about—'?" She was getting uncomfortable, her breathing shallower. "Well, I'm...you mean...me trying to tell a book by its cover?"

He sagged, relieved. "Well done. Let's get the h-hell out of here." He picked up the pillowcases, handed her one. She didn't understand. He used his to rub the banister. "Erasing fingerprints."

"Ah." She nodded. "Very good idea."

He glanced at her. "It was actually '*y-your*' idea."

"Oh." Molly stared blankly for a moment, her cartwheeling brain still processing the metaphysical surreality. "Wow." Then she realized her other hand still held the talisman. "What should we do with...?"

Matt took it. Gazed at it. "G-good question...for another day."

She nodded in agreement. He put it in his pocket, then paused, pondering.

Molly frowned. "What?"

"Advice that Thelma's Gramma gave her. About really appreciating every single day while you're actually living it."

"*Carpe diem.*" Molly squeezed his arm, concurring. "Particularly this one."

They took a grateful breath together, then hurried on down.

They finished double-wiping the banister then moved through the ghostly furniture of the ornate reception room into the marble foyer. They wiped down the inside of the door frame. Then Matt used his cloth to turn the inner knob and started opening the door.

"Wait." Molly cautioned. "When we came in...'*he*' was careful that no one saw us."

"Smart." Matt only opened the door a crack.

Molly peeked out into the night and pulled back, shaking her head. Then she noticed something in the foyer behind Matt. He turned to see an antique bronze statue of *Justice* with her eyes blindfolded. Above it, a large mirror reflected their faces looking back at them. They shared a glance. Then Molly cautiously peered out again, leaned further, checked both directions. Nodded okay.

Stepping outside beneath the colonnaded portico they saw that a light snowfall had begun. They quickly cleaned the doorknob and the exterior frame. Then they stood for the briefest moment in the doorway, took a final look inside, then at each other—breathless, amazed and thankful they'd survived, but still fearfully nervous. Matt used his cloth to ease the door closed. They hid the cloths under their coats. Molly reached out and took his hand.

Both of their hearts were pounding. They held hands tightly as they walked together down the front steps, away from the nightmare, across Eighty-Eighth Street, toward Fifth Avenue, Central Park, and into the night with the freshening flakes of snow drifting down.

From the balustrade above the portico, observing them depart, was a shadowed face. It was one of the statuary cherubs. Its smiling, stone-cold eyes seemed focused on them.

Knowing their secrets.

AUTHOR'S NOTE

*A portion of the author's proceeds
from this work goes to benefit
Doctors Without Borders
(Medecins Sans Frontieres)*

ACKNOWLEDGMENTS

This book would not exist without great help from the following friends...

Italia Gandolfo and Renee Fountain at Gandolfo Helin & Fountain Literary Management whose continued enthusiasm and guidance arranged a perfect fit for the novel with Richard Chizmar at his Cemetery Dance Publications. I'm indebted to Richard and to VP/Managing Editor Dan Franklin who shepherded me through their process.

Dan's assigning Robert Mingee was a gift. Robert brought his consummate editorial skills with a light hand and wonderful sense of humor, but also keen insights and probing questions which stirred me to assess many passages more carefully to make them the best possible.

Then Lisa Libel picked up the torch as proof editor and did a splendid super-fine-tuning of the manuscript. When I suddenly had some last-minute inspirations that unexpectedly added several new sequences Lisa had tremendous patience and graciously helped me work them through to perfection. She also had an important hand in the promotion and marketing of the book.

Looking at several graphic designers Dan suggested I was struck by the art of Kealan Patrick Burke, whom we were lucky to engage. Working from a concept I suggested, Kealan's very first pass delivered a strong, compelling book cover that was not only what I'd envisioned, but also surprised me with ingenious touches that will be Easter eggs for readers to discover.

And as ever, I am most grateful for the daily nurture, literary taste, and moral certitude of my wife Susie. She is beloved by me and all who benefit from her innate wisdom of human nature, her wise counsel, her grace -- and definitely her humor.

Throughout our entire fifty years together, Susie has been my North Star.

ALSO BY KENNETH JOHNSON

ABOUT THE AUTHOR

Kenneth Johnson, Amazon/Best-selling author of *The Man of Legends* and other novels, is also Creator/Director of such Emmy Award-winning shows as *The Bionic Woman, The Incredible Hulk, Alien Nation* and the landmark original miniseries **V** -- the highest-rated work of science fiction in television history. Johnson was nominated for the Writers Guild Award for **V** and has received multiple Saturn Awards from the Academy of Science Fiction, as well as the Sci-Fi Universe Lifetime Achievement Award and the prestigious Viewers for Quality Television Award. He and Susan, his wife of 50 years, live in Los Angeles.

www.kennethjohnson.us

 facebook.com/KennethJohnsonAuthor

www.ingramcontent.com/pod-product-compliance
Lightning Source LLC
Chambersburg PA
CBHW031953010726
47493CB00007B/2185